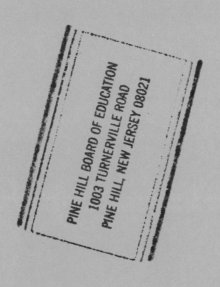

Starbright
and the
Dream
Eater

JOY COWLEY

Starbright
and the
Dream Eater

HARPERCOLLINS*PUBLISHERS*

Library of Congress Cataloging-in-Publicaton Data
Cowley, Joy.
    Starbright and the Dream Eater / Joy Cowley
        p.   cm.
    Summary: As the powerful alien life force called the Dream Eater begins to
spread destruction over the Earth, twelve-year-old Starbright discovers that she
is the one destined to stop it.
    ISBN 0-06-028419-6 — ISBN 0-06-028420-X (lib. bdg.)
    [1. Dreams—Fiction.   2. Science fiction.]   I. Title
PZ7.C83537 St   2000   99-48094
[Fic]—dc21   CIP
                                                                             AC

Typography by Al Cetta
1   2   3   4   5   6   7   8   9   10
❖
First published in New Zealand by Viking Penguin Books.
First U.S. Edition, 2000

For Miriam Marecek, the book lady

Starbright
and the
Dream
Eater

CHAPTER ONE

The nurse ran across the lawn, blowing on her hands and making breath smoke in the still night air. Already the bottom steps of the porch were white and slippery with frost. She steadied herself to look at the number on the wall of the house. Yes, this was it: two storied, in need of paint, lights behind the curtains. Far above the roofline, the sky was as dark as forever and glittering with a million stars. Somewhere distant, a dog howled, and the sound threaded itself through the street like a thin tinsel ribbon.

For months, the nurse had known about this event. Every word of the prediction had been engraved on her mind by her brother, Jacob, but now that the time was showing itself, the details came as a surprise. She clasped her bag firmly, stepped onto the porch and raised her hand.

The man opened the door before she could knock, and in an instant she was inside the hall, wrapped in warm golden light. He was a thin young man with red hair tied in a ponytail, pale freckled skin and anxious eyes. He wore a purple knitted jacket that did not suit him, and he talked in a soft hurried voice as though he were running out of words.

"She's well on the way. It's two weeks early, you understand, and Mrs. Bridgeman's out on a case. It's Mrs. Bridgeman she's been seeing."

"That's all right, Mr.—Mr. Connor. I'm Miss Tietz from the Well-Care Agency. I realize that your wife has gone into labor a little early. That's not a complication. Is there somewhere I can take off my coat—"

"Oh no!" He grasped her elbow. "Not my wife. It's Esther. Our daughter."

"Your—" She stopped, remembering the rules of the agency. No irrelevant questions or comments. All the same, the prediction had not given this information. She stared at him.

"She's fifteen," the man said. "I'm sorry, I forget my manners. Let me take your bag. I'll get a hanger for your coat. There's a bedroom off the hall if you want to change, and the bathroom's this way—"

The nurse was used to changing in a hurry. She fastened the last button of her blue-striped uniform as she followed the nervous young man up the stairs.

"Obviously the agency didn't supply all the details," she said. "The baby's father—"

"We don't know who the baby's father is," he said. "I don't think Esther knows. We don't talk about it." He looked back at her. "Esther is a uniquely gifted girl with special needs."

The nurse stopped. "She's handicapped?"

"That's not how we describe Esther," he said. "She is a girl of rare beauty. She has talents that others don't share."

They were now halfway up the stairs, and she could hear voices, one of them high-pitched and struggling with pain. She asked the question that was filling her with doubt. "Is the baby to be adopted?"

The man seemed surprised. "What?"

"I am sorry, I need to know—"

"Certainly not!" Something in his manner made him seem older, stronger. "Miss Tietz, we do not give away our own."

The nurse smiled, reassured. "I only asked because it makes a difference to the way we present the baby to the mother. We don't encourage bonding if the baby is going to another home."

"No, no! It has never been considered!" He put his hand on her shoulder and steered her toward a door at the top of the stairs. "Please hurry," he said.

It was a child's bedroom with dolls, teddy bears, a fluffy rabbit on a bookcase, a poster of white doves above the bed. The base of the bedside lamp was a clump of colored coral, and above it, fish painted on a shade turned slowly with the heat. In a chair on the other side of the bed sat a plump young woman with black hair and eyes so dark that they mirrored the room. She was holding the hand of the girl-child in the bed.

I am growing old, thought Miss Tietz. They all look impossibly young.

She introduced herself and then attended to the girl, who was tossing her head on the pillow and whimpering. Esther looked much like her mother, except that her hair was a rich auburn and her skin as freckled as the sky outside. Her eyes were narrowed in pain.

"Esther, I'm Lena Tietz, your nurse. Can I feel your tummy?" She pulled back the covers, her voice offering bright comfort. "Let's see what this fine baby is doing." Her hands, too, were confident and very gentle as they made a routine examination.

Yes, the girl was into second-stage labor and the baby was in the correct position, no apparent complications, thank goodness.

"Everything's perfect, honey," she said. "You're doing wonders."

The mother was even more nervous than the father. "Is she—I mean is everything—"

"Fine. Just fine. The baby's where it should be. Plenty of room in the birth canal." She smiled at Esther. "If all my clients were like you, I'd be a very happy nurse."

Thirty years of experience in deliveries had given Miss Tietz a manner that made childbirth a busy celebration for most mothers. A few baby jokes, and the panic in the eyes of the woman and her daughter disappeared. Esther even managed to laugh between the contractions that were coming so fast, there was scarcely a pause between them.

"There's a mighty frost outside. You'd wonder why a baby would be in a hurry to leave its warm cozy mother on such a night. But have you seen the stars, Esther?" She turned her head toward the window. "Like a fireworks display!"

At once, Mrs. Connor stood up and pulled back the curtains. The darkness beyond the window was masked by the steam inside the glass.

"A treat of a sky," the nurse said. "Whole constellations so close you could touch them."

The girl gasped, "Esther name—it—name—star."

"Absolutely, my dear," said the nurse. "Esther means star, and you're a star in every sense of the word. Isn't that right? Now give a big push."

Mrs. Connor stood on her chair, to wipe the top half of the window with a towel. Beyond the glow of the tropical-fish lamp, pinpoints of light were smeared against the black wetness of the pane. As she stepped down from the chair, she said in a soft voice, "Esther was born in a hospital and a forceps delivery went wrong. Her skull was fractured—"

The nurse nodded in understanding.

"We nearly lost her," whispered Mrs. Connor. "I'm worried. She's two weeks early and the doctor is away. Perhaps we should call an ambulance."

"Nothing will go wrong, I promise," said the nurse. She wanted to add that she knew because she had prior knowledge, but instead, she leaned over the girl. "Esther, will you turn your head to the window? Look at the stars out there. See how beautiful they are? You're the star now. You're bright and powerful, the biggest star in the sky. When that feeling in your tummy comes again,

I want you to hold your breath and push as hard as you can. Can you do that?"

"Bright star bright," grunted the girl. "Esther name—"

"It's coming. Push down into your tummy, Esther. A strong push, my fine big star. Keep pushing. That's the way."

For more than half an hour, her voice guided the girl through the wrenching contractions.

"That was very good, Esther. We'll get your mother to rub your back some more. There. Does it feel better?"

Esther's hair was lank with sweat, her face flushed, her eyes dull. She was growing tired.

"Push, Esther, push! Your baby's nearly here."

The girl whimpered, "Esther can't, can't—"

"You can. Come on now, a deep breath and a big push, big, big—that's it. Wonderful!" Nurse Tietz smiled. "I can see the baby's head, Esther. It has dark hair. All right, you can stop pushing, now. Light panting breaths, in and out like this—hah-hah-hah. Easy does it, honey."

Moments later, a fine baby girl came headfirst into the world, wet, slippery as an eel. The infant did not cry but blinked and flailed her arms as though searching for something to hold. Her face had a folded look, like the wings of a newly hatched butterfly, but, even so, she strongly resembled her mother and grandmother. Her thick black hair was plastered against her scalp; her pink lips opened and closed, opened and closed.

With quick hands, the nurse checked the infant—airways, breathing, heart, reflexes. Yes, she was perfect in every detail. Nurse Tietz put the baby on Esther's chest and covered them both with a soft cotton blanket.

"She's beautiful!" the girl cried. "Look, Mumma! A baby, a girl. It's a baby girl, so beautiful, Mumma."

"Like you, Esther. Oh sweetheart, she's the image of you when you were born." Mrs. Connor was laughing and weeping and kissing her daughter. "You brilliant, darling girl. Just wait until your poppa sees her."

Mr. Connor came back in wearing a worried look that changed to wonder as he approached the bed. He knelt with his wife beside their daughter, and Miss Tietz smiled as she looked at the three faces together, young man, young woman, adolescent girl, all bent over the new life and glowing like candle flames. She felt a deep satisfaction. It was going well. If what they said was true, there was hope yet for the world.

"The baby didn't cry," Mrs. Connor said.

The nurse read her concern. "There's not a thing wrong with her. Some babies do and some don't. Depends if they like what they see. This one is an old soul. Look at that face. I reckon she knows more than any of us. What are you going to call her?"

"We decided on Rose," Mrs. Connor said.

"Starbright," said Esther, not taking her eyes from the baby.

The nurse sucked in her breath and did not dare speak.

"Starbright?" Mr. Connor leaned back as though distance would make a difference to the name. "Why Starbright? Didn't you say you liked Rose for a girl and Ben for a boy?"

"No, Starbright," Esther said. "Esther like Starbright, like star. Like star Esther."

Mrs. Connor smiled and nodded. "It's a pretty name," she said.

Miss Tietz softly released her breath. "Indeed, it is," she said.

A little before dawn, the nurse stood beside her car outside the house, waiting for the engine to warm sufficiently to defrost her windshield. The car roof shone with white crystals as deep as her finger-nails, and exhaust fumes hung in the air in a solid cloud. Although there was a faint grayness over the horizon, the light of the stars had not diminished. They pulsed out some enormous silent song against the blackness.

She got in the car and turned the heater on to the windshield.

The child was not what she had expected. She thought it would be a boy, two parents, scientific or military background. Her brother had not said any-thing about a girl born to an intellectually disabled teenager, and the description Bright Star had given no indication of gender.

Gradually, the ice on her windshield melted and she could see, through the hole, a school bus com-ing down the street.

At least, she thought, the child was in good hands. All she could do now was wait.

CHAPTER TWO

Mark was at the end of the old rail bridge, calling down to her. "Don't be an idiot, Starbright!"

She couldn't see him clearly, for the sun was directly behind him, setting fire to his hair and making haloes around his outstretched hands. She went on braiding the long elastic cords. "It's whiddly-dokey," she said. "Come and see."

But he would not step out over the river. "It's dangerous!" he yelled.

"No! The wood's really strong." She looked at the thick gray timbers between her and Mark. There were one or two gaps open to the river below, but the old bridge, closed for longer than she had known, was still sturdy enough to take a train. Mark would not walk on it because it had no sides. Sides made a difference to Mark.

"I don't mean the bridge!" he shouted at her.

She twisted the elastic cords one last time and

knotted them; then she began to wind them around her ankles. "It's easy as apple pie, Mark. Nothing can go wrong."

"This is the worst thing you've ever done in all your twelve years, Starbright Connor. I'm going to get your mumma and poppa!" He was flapping his arms up and down as though he were going to fly back to her house like a wild old goose.

She sighed and shifted on the bridge, the boards hot on the seat of her jeans. "Hoo-diddly, Mark! It's not all that high. The water's deep. If the cord does break, it'll be just like swinging out on a rope and letting go. I done that hundreds of times. You hear me, Mark?"

"Your mumma would have a fit!" he said, but he lowered his arms.

Quickly, she pulled the stretched cord around her ankles, making it as tight as she could. Most times, she thought she was lucky having Mark live next door, but they were so different that they didn't even come close to understanding each other. For as long as she could remember, Starbright had had a hankering for adventure while Mark was just plain opposite. Why, hoo-diddly, he was so fussed about being safe that he wouldn't pick up a simple old earthworm in case it was poisonous. As for food! She couldn't count the number of times Mark had come over for dinner and Mumma's wonderful dishes had sat untouched on his plate, not even one mouthful tasted.

Starbright had stopped trying to push for change. This was how Mark was, and all she could do was work around his need for safety as best she could. She yanked on the elastic cord at both ends, testing the knot against the bridge and the other around her ankles. She grinned at him and swung her legs over the edge. "Easier than spitting up a chimney, Mark. Safer than touching an electric fence with a grass stalk."

Below, the river was as flat as mirror glass, showing the underside of the bridge, her legs, the willows on either side. Beyond, the summer fields bristled with new-mown grass, and the Coulters' black-and-white cows made a line of dominoes all the way to their milking shed. She wriggled closer to the edge and looked down at ankles tied tighter than the feet of a chicken in the market. She raised her arms to the sun.

"Starbright!" screamed Mark.

"Bungee-ee-ee!" she yelled, jumping out from the bridge.

That water rushed up toward her, splintering

like glass. Cold air filled her face. Colors separated and whirled around her head, black, white, gray, green; then they slowed and came together again, slower, slower, until the river was back in one piece and hanging an arm's length away. She thought she could reach out for a handful of water, but no, the river began to move away from her. She was on the way up. Up, up. For a moment the cord seemed to come loose. She flipped in half a somersault, then went down again. Hoo-diddly! It worked! She was a human yo-yo!

It was only when she had finished bouncing that she saw the error in her plan. She hung upside down, spinning slowly, her pigtails pointing toward the water.

"Mark?"

"You're crazy!" he shouted. "Stark, raving mad, awful, stupid crazy!"

"I can't get down," she said. "I need you to untie the cords from the bridge."

"What?"

"Please, Mark!"

"No way, Starbright. You did it. You get out of it."

Her T-shirt had come out of her jeans. She tucked it in, at the same time twisting her body to look at her feet. She thought that if she swung a bit and then did a quick bounce, she would be able to grab the cord and untie it from her ankles. By bending her legs and then kicking them straight, she pushed herself into slow circles like a pendulum. Hoo-diddly! A bamboo pole in her hand and she would be able to draw perfect circles in the water. But the blood was running to her head and making noises like an engine in her ears, and she needed to be right way up. As she swung under the shadow of the bridge, she drew her knees to her chest and grabbed the cords with both hands. Well, now, at least her head was pointing to the sky and the blood was falling away from her face to her heart, where it belonged. She hung there, holding on to the cords, looking at her ankles.

"What are you going to do now?" Mark yelled.

Plain fact was, she didn't know. Maybe she could loop the cords around her left arm, hold on that way and undo the knot with her right hand. But those wang-dangle knots had set like concrete, and the cords around her arm pulled away from her with a life of their own. Before she knew it, she was upside down again, swinging above her reflection in the river.

"Mark? Mark?"

"No!"

"You have to, Mark. Untie the bridge end."

"I'm not going on that bridge, Starbright. You hear that? Not for nothing! I'm going to do what I should have done before, get your mumma and poppa."

"Please, Mark." She swung like an apple on a string, not needing reminding that she had taken Poppa's elastic rope without asking. Well, it was just the old stretchy stuff he used for tying garden tools down on his truck, but if she had asked, he would have wanted to know why and it would have got complicated something terrible. "You don't have to walk on the bridge, Mark. You can crawl. Or sit and shuffle. Please, please, Mark! I'll give you my amethyst crystal."

"I don't want your stupid crystal!" he yelled, so angry that she knew he was going to do it.

She hung still and watched him on his hands and knees, tortoise slow on the end of the bridge. Poor Mark. His mouth would be dry. He'd be shaking and trying not to look down. She knew it, and she was filled up with concern for him.

For a while she lost sight of him, and then his head appeared above the top of the cords. He stared down at her, his face whiter than bone. "I can't reach the knot."

"Yes, you can," she called back.

"No, I can't."

"If I could, you could. You got longer arms. Why don't you lie on your stomach and put your hand over. Just one arm."

He did that. One arm, two arms, it made not a bit of difference. The knot on the bridge timber was locked as tight as the one around her ankles.

By now, her pulse was crashing like surf in her upside-down ears and she was getting a headache. She bent her knees, swung a little and then grabbed the cords to pull herself upright. Well, not exactly upright. Folded up like a pocketknife, more like it.

"Mark!"

"I'm trying, Starbright. I can't undo it."

"Forget that! Cut it!"

"What?"

"You got your knife, haven't you?"

He stared at her and his hand went back to his pocket; then he grinned and held out his pocket-knife. "Yeah!"

"Don't let it fall in the river. Just cut!"

But it wasn't as easy as that. Those wuzzling cords were practically fingerproof, knifeproof, you name it. He sawed and sawed forever before two of the strands sprang apart and she dropped, swinging on the remaining cord.

He scraped at the last strand, his knife like a fiddle bow. "You sure your poppa won't be mad at me for cutting his truck ties?"

"He'll be more mad if I die of stuffocation."

"Suffocation," said Mark.

"Suffocation is not enough blood to the head. Stuffocation is too much blood."

Mark frowned and sawed. "You shouldn't make up words all the time."

"Why not?"

"Because if everyone did that, there'd be chaos, no proper communication, just—"

There was a noise like a twig snapping, a bit of a bounce, a splash and she was in dark water filled with silver bubbles. The cold of the river took her breath away, and she came up gasping, laughing, trying to swim in the current with her legs tied together. Hoo-diddly! No use kicking. She lay like an arrow pointing downstream and struck out with her arms toward some willows hanging over the bank. The water cleared her headache, replacing it with the river's own cool smell of old leaves and mud. She grabbed the willow branches, held on and let the current swing her around into the shallows. The trailing cords caught in the trees and stretched when she tried to pull them free. Oh, Poppa, she thought, you ought to use plain old ropes on that truck of yours. But they eventually came unstuck, and she was up on the bank, her ankles mostly untied, when Mark came running through the hay stubble. He seemed greatly relieved to see her.

"You okay?"

"I swim too good to deadydrown," she told him.

"I know you swim good, but your legs were tied." He looked half angry, half ready to cry. "You and your crazy ideas."

Without a word, she handed him one end of the braided cord, and he helped her to separate the strands. She was as wet as a whole lake, and the water running from her hair got in her eyes.

"You shouldn't have jumped! Suppose the cord got round your neck. Just suppose that! I care about you, Starbright."

The way he said *care* made her narrow her eyes over her smile. Their agreement had been binding, sealed with spit on the palm and a back-to-front handshake. Friends forever but no sloppy stuff on pain of death, amen. She coiled up a strand of

Poppa's cord. "You did fine on that bridge, Mark. I could still be wuddering and jiddering up there, if you hadn't cut me down."

"Don't talk about bridges," he said. "Don't even mention the word bridge." He handed her the other coils of cord and then gave her a push. "Go on home before you get pneumonia."

No one seemed concerned about Starbright coming home sopping wet. Esther was in the kitchen. They had brought her back early from pottery school, and she was helping Mumma seal the tops on jars of blackberry jelly. Pushkin, the cat, was leaning against her legs and purring. Poppa was there too, watching the little TV on top of the fridge. When Starbright started to explain about the cords, he hushed her with a wave of his hand and got closer to the screen.

Esther licked the jelly off her fingers and put her arms around Starbright, laughing and jiggling up and down in her enthusiastic way.

Mumma said to Starbright, "Drop those old ropes and give your sister a hug."

"You're sticky," Starbright said, kissing Esther on the cheek and breathing in the warm grass scent of her skin and hair. Esther always smelled good and felt good. Her hugs sent a tingling warmth over Starbright, like warm syrup poured over a pancake.

"Esther sticky. Starbright wet!" laughed Esther, scrubbing Starbright's hair with the flat of her hand. "Wet, wet, baby!"

Starbright grinned. She was always being reminded that Esther was fifteen years older. "I fell in the river," she said.

"You what?" Mumma was suddenly at her side, wringing her hands around a dishtowel.

"I was swinging over the river. I fell in."

"Splash!" said Esther. "Splash, splash! My wet baby! Wet hair, wet pants, wet shirt."

"Simon!" Mumma was talking to Poppa. "Stanton River! Isn't it fed by a tributary from Claircomb?"

"Judy, please, I'm listening!" His face was close to the pocket-sized screen.

Mumma would not be hushed. "Starbright's been in the river. Some of that water comes from Claircomb. It could be infected."

Poppa turned off the TV and looked at Starbright with eyebrows lifted, his real serious look. "You—have—been—in—the—river?" he said, dropping each word like a marble in a pan.

"What kind of infection?" she asked. "Trout, eels, water beetles?"

No one laughed except Esther. Mumma looked at Poppa and wiped her hands some more on the towel. She said, "They've got spindle sickness at Claircomb."

"Spindle sickness?" She stared at them. "You mean *the* spindle sickness? Here?"

"Not here. Claircomb," said Esther. "No more school. No more school."

"There have been two cases, both in the same household," said Poppa. "It's not an epidemic, you understand, and there's nothing to worry our heads about. It just pays to be careful. They've put the town of Claircomb under quarantine, and no one is allowed in or out."

"No one, no one, no more school," said Esther, shaking her head.

"They've closed Esther's pottery school?" Starbright said. "But that's not in Claircomb."

"It's on the road to Claircomb, and they are being ultracareful. It won't be a long-term closure. A week or two. In the meantime, you stay away from the river. I mean that quite seriously, Starbright."

"But Poppa, spindle sickness isn't carried in

water. I could drink the whole river and I'd be okay. I read about it. Really and truthfully, cross my heart."

"We don't joke about this, Starbright," said Mumma.

Poppa said, "No one knows how the virus is carried, but the river is a connection with Claircomb. Stay away from it."

Starbright's smile fell off her face, and she turned to Esther, who was watching her with that puppy-dog look. Esther's eagerness to make her happy sometimes annoyed Starbright, but most times, like now, it made Starbright love her older sister more than anyone or anything in the world.

"I'm sorry about your school," she said to Esther. It was true. She felt a real sorrow that pinched her heart, even if Esther didn't have enough selfishness in her to be sorry for herself. Esther loved pottery school. Every day, she made the same things, beautiful blue bowls with white birds sitting on the edge. Some of the bowls were as big as actual birdbaths, while others were as small as coffee cups. When they went out walking, Esther would look in gardens and house windows to see who had bought her bird bowls, and when she found one, she would jump up and down and hooha with pleasure.

"Esther help Mumma," Esther said. "Starbright help Mumma." She tried to give Starbright a jar of warm blackberry jelly.

"No, Esther," said Mumma. "Right this minute, your sister is getting into a hot disinfectant bath. Come on, Starbright, move!"

Starbright did not argue. But why, suddenly, the big wahoo on spindle sickness? Everyone had talked for years about it, a virus disease in remote South America, then in Africa, Australia. People got tired and went to sleep and didn't wake up. How could it be here, less than thirty miles away? Nah. Wasn't possible. An outbreak would be too unreal for words. It was just someone doing a grade-A panic or an editor wanting to sell newspapers. But even so, she heeded Mumma's warnings about the river and allowed half a bottle of disinfectant to cloud her bathwater. It was only when she stepped into the bath, and felt the intense stinging, that she realized that the outsides of her ankles were rubbed raw.

CHAPTER THREE

Stanton School was so full of talk about spindle sickness that the grounds buzzed like a beehive on a summer day, kids hanging out under trees, on the steps, in the halls, their faces lit up with the kind of fear and fascination that followed a major earthquake or accident.

"Imagine boring little Claircomb, Missouri, the first in the country," said Marilyn Proctor. "The worst thing that ever happened there was Buzz Scheindler's father backed his pickup through the grocery-store window last Christmas."

"Real roadblocks!" said Jazzy. "National Guard units! My auntie Clare tried to call all yesterday, but phones were jammed busy. She could only get through at four o'clock this morning. You know what? She said a TV chopper flew in and the news crew were wearing white protection suits with gloves and masks."

Drew Prieto ran up, sliding his pack off his

shoulder, "Who is it? Who's sick in Claircomb?"

"Mr. and Mrs. Zimmerman," said Marilyn, "the really old couple living down by the bus station in the blue house with the bird feeders on the porch. They're in their eighties."

"They've never been to Argentina," said Jazzy. "Or Chile or South Africa or any of those places. Coming over here to Stanton was about as far as they ever got."

"When were they last in Stanton?" someone asked with a laugh.

No one answered.

"Well, I don't think they've got spindle sickness," said Starbright. "Hoo-diddly! At their age it can be anything. This is just a whole big scare to boost the ratings of the news channels, and in a couple of days they'll say, oops, wrong diagnosis, the Zimmermans had a stroke or pneumonia or food poisoning."

"It's definitely spindle sickness," said Mark. "It's been positively identified."

Starbright threw her braids back over her shoulders. "Yeah? How do they know? You tell me."

"They said so on TV, and they know because there's been dozens of cases in Argentina and Chile . . ." His voice faded, words swamped by her wave of disapproval. He shrugged to let her know that he didn't care what she thought.

"But how do they know the Zimmermans have it?" She went right on after him. "They haven't identified the virus yet. All these years and they still know willy-waldo about it. They don't even know that it is a virus."

"They think it comes from outer space," said Drew. "UFOs or something. I saw it on Channel Five."

"Some people say it came back on the Mars probe," said Jazzy.

"My dad thinks it's a kind of radiation sickness," said Marilyn. "You know all that nuclear waste they've got stored under mountains? It's leaking out and evaporating into the atmosphere."

Mark nodded. "For years we've been poisoning this planet. It can't take it any longer, and now it's payback time. Mother Earth is going to get her revenge on us."

Starbright glared at him. "By zapping old Mr. and Mrs. Zimmerman of Claircomb?"

That could have been the beginning of a major argument, but right in front of them, a bus pulled up and a crowd of high school kids got out: girls with wrapped hair, fluorescent lipstick and long purple nails, boys with mustaches and muscles that made their T-shirts look padded. They slouched through the gates looking like some hotshot sports team sent to perform at a kindergarten picnic.

Drew whistled and muttered, "Talk about alien invasion!"

Mark turned to Starbright as if she did not know and said, "The kids who usually get bused to Claircomb High."

And all over the school, conversation drained away as though someone had pulled a plug.

That morning, every class had its own special assembly, and Mrs. Keppler, social studies teacher—otherwise known as Mrs. Okay because her first name was Olga and she really was okay, although she frothed at the corners of her mouth when she talked fast—came into their room to tell them what was going on.

"Kids, we are making two classrooms available for the high school students who can't go to Claircomb while the quarantine is in effect. Most of the students are ex-pupils of this school, so it shouldn't be difficult for us to make them feel at home."

A groan rippled through the room, and Mrs.

Keppler smiled in understanding. She often did that, gave a smile to mean one thing when she had to say another. It was one of the characteristics that made her Mrs. Okay. Another was her habit of calling even the little kids ladies and gentlemen.

"Now, ladies and gentlemen, the National Guard Service in conjunction with the medical authorities has set up an information bureau in this area."

"What's a bureau?" someone called out.

"Like a donkey," someone else replied.

Mrs. Keppler's eyes glittered and creased. "They say that everyone will be kept well informed, which will avoid ill-founded rumor and panic." She picked up a felt pen and twirled it between thumb and forefinger. "Some of you may know that, already, at least two families have packed up and left Stanton."

It was clear no one knew that. Kids swiveled in their chairs, and a babble of alarm filled the room. Mrs. Keppler tapped the pen on the desk. "Such things happen when people have a knee-jerk reaction to gossip. All right, ladies and gentlemen, let us put aside all the rumor we have heard and write down the facts we have about spindle sickness. Can anyone tell me how it got its name?"

"'Sleeping Beauty,' Mrs. Keppler," said Marilyn.

"Thank you, Marilyn." Mrs. Keppler wrote a few

words on the board. "People went to sleep and didn't wake up. Someone thought of the fairy tale of the princess who pricked her finger on a spindle and slept for a hundred years, and the name stuck. Personally, I don't understand how that happened to the princess. A spindle is used for spinning woolen yarn, and it has no sharp parts to it. However, legends are legends and must be honored. In Argentina, where the disease first appeared, it was called *enfermedad de Corazón*. Does anyone know why?"

"It means sickness of the heart," said Marta.

"Yes, it does, but that is not the origin of the name. Corazón is the tiny village in Argentina where the first cases were reported. Can you tell me the date?"

No one could. Starbright guessed. "Maybe 1995?"

"No, Starbright. It was sometime in 1985. So you see, it has been around for a while, almost as long as you ladies and gentlemen." She wrote another sentence on the board. "Now, in the last two or three years, spindle sickness has had a lot of publicity, mainly because of the funding that's been poured into research. But—and this is important to remember—the disease is not nearly as prevalent as the media would have us believe. It will never threaten whole populations, like AIDS. Spindle sickness is serious, but I suppose we can compare it with the African disease Ebola fever in that it is localized and contained in certain areas."

"Like Claircomb," someone said, and once more a buzz broke out in the classroom.

Mrs. Keppler tapped the board. "It remains to be seen if Claircomb actually has spindle sickness. Personally, I have my doubts. Mark Dudnelly, you wish to say something?"

"It's a fact," said Mark. "It's been diagnosed."

Mrs. Keppler smiled. "We know that two residents of Claircomb were found unconscious with symptoms resembling the disease, but since no doctor here has had direct experience with spindle sickness, diagnosis is largely guesswork."

"Told you!" Starbright said to Mark.

"True diagnosis is difficult anyway," said Mrs. Keppler, white foam working at the edges of her red lipstick. "No virus has yet been isolated, and we don't know the causes. There is a theory that spindle sickness is caused by something in the environment and that certain people are susceptible to it. We do know that many of the people who get it are not in the best of health."

"Mr. and Mrs. Zimmerman are old," said Jazzy, trying to sound helpful.

Drew was rocking on his chair. "What do you think about this UFO business, Mrs. Keppler? They think the sickness is from another planet."

Everyone, including Starbright, sat up straight.

Mrs. Keppler laughed. "Exciting stuff, Andrew. You've been watching the science fiction channel. So have the rest of us. UFOs, alien invasion, people going into comas because their psyches are being whisked away to another planet. In the Middle Ages, the Black Plague was supposed to have been caused by demons let loose on earth. I am always amazed, and delighted, at the scope of the human imagination."

"These guys on TV say it's true, Mrs. Keppler," said Brett, who sat behind Drew and Jazzy. "In Argentina, there was this warning came from outer space way back in the 1970s or something."

She smiled. "When you are my age, Brett, you will look back and understand my skepticism. I suppose what it comes down to is that people believe what they want to believe. Now, let's forget science fiction and focus on factual information. What do you know about the symptoms of spindle sickness?"

"People go to sleep and die," said Mark.

"Early symptoms suggest disturbed sleep patterns," said Mrs. Keppler, scribbling fast on the board. "It seems that people can have unusual nightmares. There is increasing tiredness and lethargy. Instead of feeling refreshed after sleep, people wake up exhausted."

Marta sighed and ran her fingers through her curly black hair. "Tell me about it!" she murmured at Mrs. Keppler's back. "I get spindle sickness every Monday morning."

Starbright went out with Mark and Jazzy at morning recess and practiced shooting baskets in the school yard. Talk flew around them as they tossed the basketball to each other. Everything they said and did was watched by the big kids, who hung in groups near doorways. The others, especially the younger kids, walked wide around the teenagers, who didn't do much except scowl, although one of them, a boy with an X shaved into his hair, smoked a cigarette in front of everybody and no one stopped him. Starbright knew him. He was Dan Coulter, whose father had the dairy farm across the river. All the Coulters were as big and slow moving as the cattle they raised.

When he had squished his cigarette butt with

his shoe, Dan Coulter wandered over and snatched the basketball away from Jazzy. No one said anything. He dribbled the ball a few times, grinned at them, shot a couple of baskets, then three, four, half a dozen. Starbright walked up to Dan to ask if they could have their ball, but Mark grabbed her arm and pulled her back. Too late. Dan Coulter had noticed her. He spun the basketball on the tip of his forefinger and smiled. "You're the Connor kid."

"So what?"

"The one with the sister who's a sandwich short of a picnic."

Starbright went cold from head to foot, cold and strong as steel. She took one long step toward him and came so close that she directly faced the front of his shirt, which had a faded picture of Hercules on it. "Would you mind repeating that?" she said.

"Why?" He laughed. "You got the same problem?" He began dribbling the ball again.

"Apologize!" she demanded, ignoring Mark's hand signals. "Go on! Apologize!"

Dan Coulter stared. "What? Me apologize because your sister is fifty cents in the dollar? Why should I?"

Starbright made her hands as stiff as boards and held them in front of her face. "You galumping oxymoron! Apologize this minute or suffer the consequences!"

Dan Coulter barked with laughter, then sneered at Starbright. He grabbed the basketball in both hands and would have shoved it into her face if Mark hadn't yelled, "Don't start anything! She's got a black belt in karate!"

"Oh yeah?" Coulter laughed again. "And I'm the man in the moon."

"No kidding," said Mark. "The last guy who made fun of her sister wore a cast on his arm for six weeks."

"He sure did," said Jazzy, nodding her head as though it would come all the way off.

Dan Coulter snorted in disbelief but stepped back. He threw the ball as far as he could, and it bounced off the door of a classroom. "You kids better watch it, you hear?" he said as he walked away.

Starbright might have run after him if Jazzy and Mark hadn't closed in on her. Jazzy put her arm around her shoulders, and Mark said, "Just what were you going to do to him? Get him in a headlock? Tie his legs in knots?"

"I don't know," she said.

"One day your friends won't be around to rescue you," he said.

She knew he was talking about yesterday too, still feeling angry about the old rail bridge.

"Thanks," she murmured.

Jazzy said, "Dan Coulter's got a stupid mouth but he's okay. Ignore him, Starbright. Most times he's just trying to be funny."

"And you might as well know," said Mark, "that oxymoron is a grammatical expression. It's supposed to describe things that contradict each other."

"Like what?" said Starbright.

"Like jumbo shrimps," said Jazzy.

"Like a crash course in defensive driving." Mark grinned.

The bell sounded the end of recess, and they walked back to class. Starbright punched Mark on the arm. "Hoo-diddly! I know an oxymoron: me having a black belt in karate."

CHAPTER FOUR

Lena Tietz spread the map on the passenger seat and fingered County Road 208, the back road to Stanton that wound, like a snake, through farmland and forest. She guessed it would be a slow journey. The dirt road was designed for tractors, horses and farm trucks, but now it would be blocked like a cholesterol-ridden artery with Claircomb bypass traffic and a national collection of news vehicles.

Lena Tietz was tired, worn down by dust, heat and lack of sleep. For the three days since the Claircomb outbreak, she had been working around the clock, trying to find the Connor family. She had started the search in Bannerville, where she had attended the child's birth, only to learn that the family had moved the following year to Claircomb. She had more or less expected that. In fact, she was almost certain that the Zimmermans were in some way associated with the Connors. She hunted through the C columns in the phone book. They were not listed. Maybe they didn't have a phone. Even in this day and age, such a thing was possible, but how would she know? It would be difficult to get into the quarantined area for an on-the-ground search, especially if she wanted to get out again. She called the local National Guard alert and told them she was a nurse worried about some patients who lived in Claircomb. Without too many questions, they faxed her a printout of their list of Claircomb residents. It surprised her. There was not one Connor in the entire town of 3,763 persons, no Connor child at any of the three schools. At this point her search could have become very difficult, had she not looked at a list of closed facilities in outlying areas. There it was, seventeen miles out of Claircomb, a community college with courses for persons with special needs. Listed in the ceramics class was the name of the child's mother, Esther Connor, 7 Second Street, Stanton.

Lena Tietz picked up her tumbler, rattled the ice cubes in her lemonade and wondered what she was going to say to the family. Where was the first thread she could pull to unravel such a complex and extraordinary tale? She herself had decided not to believe it. For years she had dismissed her brother Jacob's growing files of evidence, because belief meant a burden too heavy to carry. She had excused herself by accusing others. She told herself that the astronomer Eduardo Camino de Cruz, and the UFO Society that supported his claims, had a comic-book mentality. She said they confused astronomy with astrology and hocus-pocus superstition. She would have added a mouthful about Jacob Tietz, writer, linguist, journalist with a special interest in the shamanic religions of the American continents. In fact, she would have judged him completely crazy had he not been her dearly beloved twin. Instead, she told him he was naive.

"Jacob," she had said, "it's people like you who provide full-time employment for confidence tricksters."

He had smiled at her as though he were humoring a child. "Lena, you do not have to believe. It will come to you because we are the twins of the prophecy. We are like the prophets of old. Jeremiah, Isaiah, Jonah. They all wanted to run away from God, and much good it did them. Now, Lena, don't roll your eyes like that. You don't believe in God? Okay, okay, names are not important. Trust the universe, then. The universe knows what it is doing.

4¹

You will bring the Bright Star into the world."

Poor Jacob! She had shaken her head in wonderment at his persistent attempts to involve her in his insanity. Deliver a baby? Hah! She had retired from babies four years before and was working for a nursing agency. Her clients were mainly elderly, and her work involved removing sutures, changing dressings, giving antibiotic shots, making notations of any irregularity that needed the attention of a doctor. Jacob and his space-invasion theory had been far from her mind that winter night over twelve years ago. She had left a client's house and was sitting in her car with the light on, writing up her notes, when the car phone rang. It was the Well-Care Agency. A young Bannerville woman was in advanced labor. Would Miss Tietz please pick up an obstetrics bag at the doctor's clinic and proceed promptly to the following address?

That was when the change came. It was not so much like a religious conversion as a fast rolling of wheels in a slot machine, Jacob's words, figures and diagrams whirling in her head and then settling, *clunk, clunk, clunk, clunk.*

Later, she and Jacob had checked the coordinates with a small handheld global positioning system. The figures sent in 1979, from a galaxy too far away to be measured in light-years, to an Argentinian village too small to be taken seriously, were so accurate that they came within plum-pit-spitting distance of Esther Connor's bed.

Lena Tietz wound up the car window. She had been right about both the road and the traffic. The views of green fields and forests were mostly hidden by clouds of white dust that had been made into flour by the constant hammering of wheels. She did not see cars full of news teams. No doubt they were there in the solid lines of traffic. But she did meet at least four moving vans and one truck piled high with table, chairs, bed headboards, plastic buckets, everything coated with road dust.

I don't blame them, she thought. If I were a farmer living here, I'd probably be moving out too. But what is the point? According to the prediction, in five years there will be no place left to run to.

The thought brought Lena Tietz back to the present moment and the enormity of the task in front of her. What was she going to say to a nice normal couple, their special twenty-seven-year-old daughter and a twelve-year-old granddaughter whom Lena had not seen since birth? Did she walk right up and knock on the door? "Excuse me, this child has been given the job of saving the world because a voice from outer space said so."

She sighed and picked up her lemonade to rinse away the dust in her throat. Her brother would say to her: Trust in the universe. All his life he had held the belief that if you simply stepped out and did what your conscience told you to do, the universe would take care of the details. But faith and dedication did not always work, not even for her dear trusting brother. She felt the burning return to her eyes, and she took off her glasses, wiped tears with the back of her hand. At this very minute Jacob was in a hospital in Melbourne, Australia, dosing on amphetamines to try to stay awake.

The house was different from the birthplace at Bannerville, but of the same vintage and state of repair. The paint on the walls of the bungalow was peeling on the sunny side, and the roof of the porch looked as though an elephant had sat on it. The yard, though, was quite lovely, with beds of lavender and petunias, and fat roses hanging like balls of snow over pottery birdbaths decorated with thrushes and doves. She paused beside them, remembering the community college and the ceramics course. Was this Esther Connor's work? Delicate glazes?

Plump-breasted birds that bathed their wings or else reached up, ready to fly into an admirer's hand? She would have looked closer, but then she glimpsed a man in the driveway, unloading a concrete mixer from the back of a pickup truck that was painted with a sign: SIMON AND JUDY CONNOR, ORGANIC GARDENING. Ah yes, it was he, twelve years older, in blue overalls with ginger hair, short now and balding on top, but face and body just as thin, his wrists knobbly, his arms more bone than muscle.

"Mr. Connor?"

He smiled at her across the bed of the truck.

"I'm Lena Tietz," she said.

The name meant nothing to him. Why did she think he would remember? He nodded slightly, his smile polite and unquestioning. "Judy's in the kitchen," he said. "Go on in."

She knew he had assumed that his wife was expecting her, and she stayed on the back porch, knocking softly until Judy Connor heard. She too had changed, but not as much as her husband. Her hair was long and dark, her skin smooth and pale, her arms as plump as his were thin. She smiled less in greeting and more in inquiry.

"Mrs. Connor, you may remember me. I'm Lena Tietz—"

She stared and her brow wrinkled slightly. "I'm sorry—"

Lena spoke warmly. "You used to live in Bannerville. You have a daughter Esther—"

"Yes?" The frown deepened.

"Mrs. Connor, I was the nurse who attended Esther. Nurse Tietz. I was there because Esther's nurse and doctor—"

Judy Connor's eyes opened wide. "Oh!" she said. "I'm sorry, I'm afraid we are busy."

Lena Tietz put an arm and a foot in the doorway, coming so close to the woman that she could feel the movement of her breath. "I'd like to talk—"

"Please, don't!" She flapped her hands in panic. "You'll have to leave. Simon? Simon?"

Almost instantly, the husband was on the porch looking from one to the other. Then his eyes became still. "The nurse," he said in a flat voice.

Lena pleaded. "Mr. Connor! Mrs. Connor! I have to talk to you about your granddaughter, Starbright. This is extremely complex and urgent."

"Tell her to go, Simon!" the woman cried.

"I'm sorry," he said to Lena. "That's behind us now. We have nothing to say to you. Please move out of our doorway."

She took a step backward and he pushed past her.

Lena Tietz felt weak with frustration. So much for having the universe on her side, she thought. She grabbed the man's wrist. "Believe me, I am not insane when I say this is a matter of life and death. Your life. Mine! There are things you don't know, but I've got all the evidence with me. It will take time. Please! It's imperative that we talk. Where is your granddaughter, Starbright?"

But they were staring at her as though she were about to murder them. The man pulled his hand away, stepped in front of his wife and slammed the door shut. She heard the click of the lock.

With knotted fists, she bashed at the door. "Give me a chance to explain!" she yelled. "Mr. Connor? Mrs. Connor? You lived in Claircomb in the Zimmermans' house, didn't you?"

There was no reply.

She parked on Main Street, Stanton, and walked over to a coffee shop, not because she was hungry but because she was tired of driving around in circles and she needed a place to think. She took a cup of coffee and a chicken sandwich across the room and sat down at a wobbly table adorned with a pink silk carnation and a ketchup bottle. On the wall above her, a TV belted out dregs of news connected with the Zimmermans. They were now down to interviewing anyone who had ever known the elderly couple. "They were just ordinary folk like us," cried a young man who filled the screen. "What did they do to deserve it? And why Claircomb? Answer me that! How come the only spindle virus in the country gets landed smack bang in the middle of Claircomb?"

Lena sipped her coffee. "I'll tell you why, buddy," she muttered to herself. "Because this is no virus. It's a life form so advanced that its intelligence makes a computer look like an abacus. It knows the prophecy, and it didn't jump over here to look for food, buddy. It's hunting for the Bright Star."

CHAPTER FIVE

Starbright was as interested as anyone in news of the Claircomb outbreak, but there wasn't enough information to fill up twenty-four hours a day. You got deadnut sick and tired of hearing the same things over and over: how many people were leaving town, the falling price of real estate in Stanton with no real estate agents left to sell it. Hoo-diddly! The rest of the world could be shaking itself to pieces big time, and there was the TV showing Mr. Zimmerman's empty boots by his backyard steps.

Mrs. Keppler told the class that, after four days in the hospital, Mr. and Mrs. Zimmerman were in deep sleep but with some brain movement. Doctors could tell from electrodes planted on people's skulls how deeply unconscious they were, and the Zimmermans were still dreaming. When the brain movement slowed down, people got into the gray stage of the illness and were put on life-support

49

systems to keep their lungs and hearts going.

There were no new cases reported, but every morning people talked about their dreams the way they examined their faces in mirrors for pimples.

Of all the kids in their gang, it was Mark who was most worried.

"But you always get scarifying nightmares," said Starbright. "What's new?"

"This was really the pits," he said. "These guys with guns were chasing me, and when I hid in a thick forest, the trees shrank into tiny little stunted thin bushes they could see right through. I woke up with my heart beating so loud, it was like someone banging on the wall by my bed."

"You woke up," Starbright said. "With spindle nightmares, people have problems getting out of the dream."

Drew grinned at Mark. "That wasn't your heart banging. The guys with guns followed you out of the dream, and they were firing through your bedroom wall—*ack-ack-ack-ack-ack!*" He squinted along his finger.

"Ha, ha," said Mark. He turned back to Starbright. "Who was your visitor?" he asked.

"What visitor?" Starbright said.

"Yesterday. The lady who was shouting at

your mumma and poppa."

"Who?" Starbright thought that maybe he was describing another part of his nightmare.

"Didn't they tell you?"

"Mark Dudnelly, what are you talking about?"

"Mom told me. She was out in the yard and she heard raised voices, your mumma, another lady, then your poppa. So she looked over the fence. You know, just in case there was some kind of trouble and they needed help. Your mumma and poppa closed the door on this lady, but she was set on staying there, knocking and calling out."

Starbright shrugged. "Probably trying to sell something."

"Mom said she was asking them about the Zimmerman house," said Mark. "Your folks lived in Claircomb, didn't they?"

"For a little while when I was a baby."

"Was it the same house as the Zimmermans'?"

Starbright tried to remember if her parents had mentioned that. Maybe they had, maybe they hadn't. She tended to forget things that didn't interest her. "I don't know."

"That woman!" said Drew. "She must be the same one as on our street. How old was she?"

"Mom said old," Mark replied. "Gray hair and glasses."

Drew hunched his shoulders and spread his hands. "Different. But maybe there's a whole bunch of them at it. Going from door to door telling people the spindle sickness has come because people turned their backs on God. Like the angel of death visiting Egypt, they reckon. Real morbid stuff."

Jazzy came in fast, looking at the clock. Her hair was different this morning, oiled, braided and threaded with fine Moroccan money beads, but her face looked as heavy as a wet day.

"You okay, Jasmine?" Drew called.

She flapped a hand at him as she dropped her books on her desk. "Don't ask!" she said. "I just had the most awful dream!"

"Join the club," said Mark.

"No kidding around," she said. "My bed was full of spiders, and I didn't know if I was waking or dreaming, it was so real. When I finally did wake up, I was too scared to go back to sleep again." She turned to Starbright. "You ever do that?"

"Starbright doesn't get nightmares," Mark said.

"No?" said Jazzy.

Starbright felt embarrassed. She scrunched her mouth and didn't reply.

"No bad dreams at all?" Jazzy insisted.

Starbright wriggled her shoulders with embarrassment. "My sister doesn't get them either. My poppa does. Sometimes he yells in his sleep. Every now and then Mumma dreams the house is on fire."

"So how come you and Esther avoid your own horror movies?" said Jazzy. "Any formula I should know?"

Starbright shrugged again. It seemed downright insensitive for her to go glagging and hupping about the way she enjoyed her dreams, which were, on the whole, better than any movie or book adventure. She said, "You can sort of control them, you know. If there are spiders, turn yourself into a big bird and chase the spiders away. If you are falling, grow wings. People after you? Dream up some rope and lasso them. Turn their guns into balloons and make them float out of sight."

"Oh, sure!" said Mark, and everyone groaned.

"Starbright, that's trash," said Drew.

"You asked," Starbright said.

"Spiders, yeah, yeah," said Mark. "But what about cockroaches? Huh? A big, fat, juicy cockroach?"

Starbright put her hands over her ears. "Shut up, Mark!"

"What did it," said Jazzy, "was my hair. This braiding took four hours last night, and while I was getting it done, I ate a Supremo double cheese pizza like it was going out of fashion."

"Cheese!" cried Drew. "Serves you right, Miss Piggy!"

Everybody, including Jazzy, laughed and threw their arms in the air and slapped each other, while Mark crowed, "Four hours of pizza!"

What's the big joke? Starbright wondered. It wasn't all that wheezling funny.

By lunch there was some fresh news buzzing around the school, as welcome as the latest pop hit. Someone had discovered that three weeks before, Mr. and Mrs. Zimmerman had gone to the wedding in Claircomb of a great-grandniece and had drunk some red Chilean wine imported from the spindle sickness area. Other wedding guests were not affected by the wine, but the Zimmermans were by far the oldest guests at the wedding. Their immune systems had been unable to cope with the spindle sickness virus.

"There you go!" Starbright said to Drew. "So much for the UFO theory. Virus on the grapes, grapes in the bottle, bottle shipped to Claircomb, one, two, three."

"I'm off wine for life," said Drew.

"Remind me not to eat any grapes, either," Jazzy said.

Mrs. Keppler told them that government vehicles were going around the country, inspecting liquor stores for stray bottles of Chilean wine, packing them in foam containers and taking them to central testing laboratories. Residents were asked to inspect their wine supplies, their food cupboards. Imports from certain regions of South America had been banned for more than a year, but there were still some food and drink items around, especially wine.

"Guess what! Next week they're going to lift the quarantine roadblocks." Jazzy wagged her head so that her beads sang and danced, sang and danced.

Good, thought Starbright. Esther could return to pottery school. Poppa and Mumma could get back to the gardens they tended over in Claircomb, and Stanton people, who'd flown off like winter swallows, could just widdle-loop around and bring their vans full of couches and fridges and TVs back to their old homes. FOR SALE signs would disappear, and so would all the high school kids who had invaded their school. Life would be normal again.

That's what Starbright thought in words, but it

wasn't the feeling she had inside her. The feeling was new, but it was growing bigger than anything that had come over the TV news. It crouched within her like a lion, shaking its head and saying that it was not nearly over. In fact, it hadn't even started. She listened to this new feeling, curious, but neither excited nor afraid. Where was it coming from, and what did it mean?

That afternoon, when she went out of the school gate and saw the woman standing on the sidewalk, the lion feeling stood up and roared right there in the middle of the sidewalk. It had to be the same woman who had gone to her home. The conversation with Mark and Drew crossed her mind, gray hair and glasses, preaching lady, selling door to door, but the lion flicked the words away like flies, and with rippling muscles, it walked toward the woman as though it had always known her.

"Starbright Connor?"

The eyes behind the woman's glasses were of an unusual color, light brown flecked with green and younger than the rest of the face, which looked like cardboard left out in the sun. The hair was steel gray, frizzy, growing out sideways, and the woman was holding a yellow envelope against her pink blouse.

"Yes."

The woman smiled, closed her eyes for a second and took a deep breath.

"I am so glad to find you. My name is Lena Tietz and we have met before, although you will not remember. I was the nurse who attended your birth."

"Really?" Starbright almost laughed. "You know, I had this feeling when I looked at you, like—like—"

The woman leaned forward, eyes alert. "Like?"

"Like I had seen you from somewhere before," said Starbright.

The woman's eyes did not leave her face. "I was the first person to see you, but I didn't know if you were still called Starbright. At your birth, your grandparents had the name Rose for you. Your mother wanted Starbright because it was like Esther, and it was such a starry night—"

"My grandparents?" said Starbright. "What were they doing there?"

"They didn't tell you? You were not born in a hospital. It was a home birth. I was called because Esther's doctor and nurse were away and your grandparents—"

"Esther is my sister," said Starbright.

The woman dropped the yellow envelope. It

slid across the sidewalk like a flat stone on water.

Starbright picked it up and handed it to her. "Sorry, Mrs.—"

"Lena Tietz."

"Mrs. Tietz, my mother—"

"It's actually Miss Tietz, but I'd like you to call me Lena."

"Well, okay, but are you sure you've got the right family? My parents are Simon and Judy Connor, and I have an older sister called Esther. That's all of us, except for our cat, Pushkin."

The woman's eyes moved back and forth across Starbright's face as though she were reading a book at high speed, and Starbright was aware that, on the other side of the school gate, Jazzy and Marilyn were waiting for her, alert with curiosity.

"I'm sorry if I'm the wrong person," she said.

"No, no. You are the right person," said Lena Tietz. "It is I who made the mistake. I am very sorry. So many mothers and grandmothers and babies over the years." She gave a small laugh. "You are Starbright Connor, born in Bannerville the sixth of December, 1986."

Starbright nodded.

"Starbright, I have something I would like you to read." She held out the envelope. "It's a copy of a magazine article published three years ago. The byline is a pseudonym, but it was written by someone I know very well, and I can swear that every word of it is true. Please read it somewhere private. I'd rather you didn't show it to anyone else."

Starbright took the envelope. "What's it about?"

"It concerns you," the woman said. "Why you were born, why you are here. I have many things to tell you, Starbright. But first I want you to read the article. We'll talk about it tomorrow. I'll wait here by the school, same place, same time."

Starbright examined the envelope. It was thick but blank on the outside. She shrugged and her thoughts said, Nutcase! But the deep lion feeling stood up straight watching for something. Or, maybe, it was waiting.

"Remember," said the woman, "it is utterly confidential."

"Sure."

Starbright turned away, hugging the envelope, but after a few steps she stopped and looked at Miss Lena Tietz, who was getting into a small green car. "Esther is my sister," she said again.

CHAPTER SIX

Starbright sat cross-legged in the middle of the old bridge and opened the envelope. This was her private thinking place, the high throne that lifted her above the small valley of Stanton. She could not see her street from here, but there was a distant view of the trees outside the school, the town hall, the bus shelter and the library, buildings all as small as in a model train layout. The farms of the valley were checkered green and gold, with houses, sheds and hay barns sitting like chess pieces waiting for a game. She shut her eyes for a moment and breathed in the smells that hung in the warm afternoon air, scents of red clover and cut summer grass, steamy hairy cows and their droppings, old wood, rusted iron, the cool whispering smell of the water. She opened her eyes. The Stanton

River wound away to narrowness until it disappeared in a thin line of willow trees at the far end of the valley. The river was why the farms and town were here. You could say that the river was the mother of Stanton.

Starbright scratched the back of her neck and thought of the things the woman had said about Esther. What a loopy-loop mix-up!

That afternoon, Mumma had taken Esther to Mrs. Morse for a dress fitting. It was being bought with Esther's pottery money, and Mumma had helped her choose the material, red silk that shone and flowed like water. Poppa was out doing the post office gardens. Mark was at brass band practice. Starbright had left a note on the kitchen table for Mumma and Esther and a phone message for Mark. Then she had come to the bridge to be alone with the envelope.

The pages inside had been photocopied from a magazine called *True Sightings*, dated September 13, 1992. There was a darkly blurred picture of a square building and an inset, also blurred, of a round lump of rock. Starbright leaned over the pictures, trying to understand them, while the lion feeling inside her grew with an eagerness that surprised her.

COUNTDOWN
Fact or Fiction?

IS SPINDLE SICKNESS A NEW
AND DEADLY FLU VIRUS?
OR IS IT CAUSED
BY AN ALIEN LIFE FORM?
ARE WE FACING THE END OF TIME?

OUR CORRESPONDENT "GEMINI" TELLS
A STARTLING TALE OF EXTRATERRESTRIAL
INVASION AND GOVERNMENT COVER-UP.
SEE PAGE 17 OF THIS ISSUE.

Starbright turned to the next page, which had
the **CO** of **COUNTDOWN** as the body of a
comet with the rest of the word tailing behind it in
a dramatic heading. Underneath was a note:

THE EDITORS OF *TRUE SIGHTINGS*, WHO KNOW
THE IDENTITY OF "GEMINI," HAVE NO REASON
TO DOUBT THE EVENTS DESCRIBED
IN THE FOLLOWING JOURNAL.

February 3, 1979: El Único Observatory, Montana Rosa, Buenos Aires, Argentina

The third of February begins as an un-exceptional day with a bright-blue sky over the new Galileo SP 300 radio telescope, which sits unattended in the observatory while a maintenance worker cleans a window in the corridor outside. A minute later, the worker congratulates a staff member on the new tele-scope that can "write by itself." The staff mem-ber, Jorge Mendoza, is puzzled. What does the worker mean? He investigates, and then Professor Eduardo Camino de Cruz is notified. The Galileo telescope is indeed "writing by itself." The writing consists of waves inscribed by a needle that is moved by a receptor almost a million times more sensitive than a seismo-graph, a receptor designed to pick up radio waves from deep space. The astronomers stand around the glass case watching in awe as the faint lines emerge on the paper. The key staff of the observatory are hypertensive with excite-ment, but they do not know they are witness-ing a disaster warning from a future time warp too many millennia away to count.

February 5, 1979: Worldwide

The radio communication to Argentina from deep space makes world news headlines. At the same time, leading astronomers from SETI (Society for Extra-Terrestrial Intelligence) in the United States, Russia, England and France deny that it is communication from an intelligent source. They state that the so-called signal is due to abnormal sunspot activity. The position of the sun over the southern hemisphere, and the sensitivity of the new telescope, give the Buenos Aires observatory a unique advantage in recording the flares.

February 8, 1979: Buenos Aires

Professor Eduardo Camino de Cruz of El Único Observatory appears on national television in Argentina. He does not accept the sunspot theory, and he is angry at what he calls the unscientific dismissal of the signals received. The solar flares are ongoing, he says, whereas the signals he received on 1420 megahertz are not. They came on the morning of February 3, two similar messages fifteen minutes apart, each message lasting three and a half minutes. Not only were the signals alike, there were, within each signal, repeated patterns that suggest organized language.

During the interview, Professor Camino de Cruz attacks his critics, accusing them of professional jealousy and claiming that they have orchestrated a plot to discredit him. Some of his statements are feared to be slanderous. The interview closes abruptly and does not make its way into world news.

The belief persists that on February 3, 1979, the Galileo telescope at El Único Observatory has picked up nothing but abnormal solar activity.

The photocopying was fainter on the next page, and Starbright had to move it out of the shadow made by her head, into bright sunlight. So far, the article wasn't all that interesting. People were always writing about flying saucers or messages from outer space, and some could make it sound a whole lot more exciting than this. She looked down at the dark water of the river and saw her own reflection haloed with rays of sunlight. "Hi, Starbright!" she said. "How's the virus down there?"

May 6, 1980: Buenos Aires

For two months, Eduardo Camino de Cruz has been working in conjunction with three sound engineers at a deaf institute in the capital, and on this day, for the first time, they hear the signals converted to sound. The electronic translation does not resemble a human voice, and although certain patterns can be recognized in the noise, the signals are more like atmospheric static than language.

May 27, 1980: Cuzco, Peru

The author, "Gemini," linguist and reporter with *The Washington Post*, has been in Peru researching the history of shamanism in South America. In a meeting that seems like chance, he hears about Professor Camino de Cruz and his ongoing attempts to decode the Galileo message. He phones the professor and, before the day is out, has booked an air ticket to Buenos Aires.

June 19, 1980: Buenos Aires

Professor Camino de Cruz with "Gemini" makes a new discovery. The Galileo message, transcribed at 25 percent of its recorded speed, is in the Kakan language of the ancient Diaguita Indians of South America. It appears to contain some kind of warning, written in a poetic form similar to that of the legends of the Diaguita people. It tells of a meteor bringing a new life form that will destroy all life on earth. It tells also of a child born with a gift that may possibly defeat the invader:

Hear this, O blue planet, a warning from the Guardians of the Universe. The heart of the Dream Eater, imprisoned in the rock, will come to rest in the heart of the blue planet, where it will be released by the Star Gazer. Yet small and seeking nourishment, the Dream Eater will shelter in halls of southern ice and stretch forth its arms to the sleep of those who know fear. Gaining entry to dreams, it will disarm its hosts with terror and devour life energy, growing larger until it encompasses the blue planet, becoming the only life force in existence. Then the one will divide to become many and seed itself into the universe, leaving behind a dead planet.

This has been foretold.

Know, however, that the All of existence is in perfect symmetry. Every destruction is balanced by creation, and the advent of a sickness is always accompanied by the arrival of a possible cure. There will be born of rare human beauty a child without fear, known as the Bright Star, who will have the potential to form a second path. The twins who serve life will serve the Bright Star and will bring her to the Eater of Dreams. The Bright Star will be given a force that may overcome the Dream Eater, if she knows how to use it well. But such is the all-seeing of her adversary, her chances of success are slight, which is why, in the spiral of universal time, the second path is known as the lesser possibility. . . .

Starbright read that bit again. What the wuzzle-doo did they mean by two possibilities? From the edge of her vision, she saw a scuttling movement over the dry timber of the bridge. Cockroach! Cockroach! Yeech! It had gone under the envelope! She couldn't help herself—she shied away from it! Then, very carefully, she lifted up the corner of the yellow envelope. She laughed. Hoo-diddly, it was only a little brown beetle wandering far from home. She went back to the page in her lap. There were dates in the message, degrees of latitude and longitude. She skipped over them to the next journal entry.

June 23, 1980: Buenos Aires

The Galileo message is formally examined by the Astrophysical Research Unit and the Society for Extra-Terrestrial Intelligence. The warning is judged to be a hoax. Professor Camino de Cruz reluctantly accepts the verdict, unable to explain why a signal from deep space should be in an extinct Indian dialect. Equally puzzling is the source of the signal. The professor suspects that a radar-jamming device has been adapted by envious colleagues and used to deliver a false message. He makes his anger public. There are threats of lawsuits on both sides, and then the Galileo incident fades from the news. "Gemini" flies back to Washington to write a series of articles on South American indigenous religions. In El Único Observatory, the files on the Galileo signals are locked away in a cabinet and forgotten by most of the staff.

March 21, 1984: The village of Corazón, 127 miles south of Buenos Aires

At 10:04 A.M. there are sharp earth tremors that cause damage to buildings in the small town of Corazón. Later, people report scorched vegetation and a deep crater a few miles to the east of the village. The time, date and location of the crater's appearance are exactly those predicted in the recorded Galileo signal.

March 23, 1984: Corazón

Professor Eduardo Camino de Cruz, two of his staff and a team of maintenance workers from the observatory travel to Corazón, set up camp by the crater and begin excavations.

March 25, 1984: Corazón

A meteorite is unearthed in the crater. It is of a regular round shape and about the size of a child's head, composed of a dark-gray meta-morphic substance unlike any geological specimens in the area. There is a possibility that the meteorite contains a new element unknown on earth.

March 26, 1984: 11:00 A.M.

The professor receives official notice that the meteorite is the property of the Instituto Geológico Nacional de Argentina and that his intervention is considered as trespass. He is told that he must replace the rock in the crater and wait until a government party of geologists arrives in two days' time.

March 26, 1984: 2:30 P.M.

Professor Eduardo Camino de Cruz leaves Corazón with the meteorite packed in Styrofoam in the back of a van. He is by himself. His staff do not see him again.

April 3, 1984: Washington, DC

"Gemini" receives an urgent phone call from Jorge Mendoza from El Único Observatory. Professor Camino de Cruz has disappeared with the meteorite and is wanted by the police. There has also been an explosion and a fire at a research station near the Chilean border. No one survived the fire, and only one body is identified, that of a female laboratory assistant.

Now, Professor Camino de Cruz's wife has given Jorge Mendoza a film that her husband mailed to her the morning before the explosion. The film has been developed. There are photos of the meteorite, photos of the laboratory. Undoubtedly, the professor was killed in the explosion, although officially, he is thought to be in North America. Mendoza goes to the burned-out research station and finds particles of the meteorite, which confirm his belief.

"Gemini" wants to fly immediately to Buenos Aires, but Mendoza warns him that he will almost certainly be arrested. There is a rumor in Buenos Aires that "Gemini" has conspired with Camino de Cruz to sell the valuable meteorite to the U.S. government.

Mendoza sends "Gemini" copies of the photographs.

October 15, 1985: Washington, DC

"Gemini" receives a call from Jorge Mendoza, who says that there is a strange illness in the town of Corazón, people falling asleep and not waking up. In Washington, "Gemini" buys a ticket to fly to Buenos Aires but discovers at the airport that his visa has been revoked.

March 19, 1986: Washington, DC

"Gemini" receives a letter telling him that Mendoza is dead, a victim of the new sickness. It is thought that the disease is caused by a new strain of bacillus in the drinking water, but no one is sure. Again "Gemini" tries to go to Argentina, and again he is refused entry.

March 20, 1986: Washington, DC

A package arrives for "Gemini" from Jorge Mendoza, mailed almost three weeks before

Mendoza's death. It contains copies of all the files on the Galileo signals plus the meteorite particles taken from the charred wreckage of the research station.

March 21, 1986: Florida

"Gemini" takes a leave from his position with *The Washington Post* to do full-time research on the Galileo message. He thinks he now understands why the message arrived in an obscure Indian dialect. The intelligence that relayed the warning probably did so through some laser-computer network that used the language of the place where the meteorite would land. It also used the poetic idiom of that language. It would have no way of knowing that the Indians who had spoken the language had died out. "Gemini" has the theory that Professor Camino de Cruz, in trying to destroy the meteorite, actually released the life form held inside it. It is possible that this life form, which the warning calls the Dream Eater, is so foreign to life known on earth that it cannot be detected by ordinary human perception.

March 28, 1986: Florida

Now "Gemini" has all the information on computer and is sending printouts to newspaper and magazine editors, senators, medical research centers, members of parliaments the world over. The reception he gets is either silent or coolly polite, although the medical profession begins to take a serious interest in the strange sleeping sickness that is affecting the southern latitudes.

April 4, 1986: Florida

The UFO Society interviews "Gemini." They move to set up an international grid to monitor the predictions and the progress of the new illness.

May 28, 1986: Florida

"Gemini" is now getting weekly reports from the UFO Society, and he notes that there is a steady escalation in the illness. Dozens of cases have been reported in Argentina, a number in Chile, and three in Cape Town, South Africa. From the predictions, "Gemini" makes the following assumptions:

1. The Dream Eater is a parasite. It is an

intelligent being in energy form, which feeds off living energy.

2. The Dream Eater does not appear to reproduce sexually. It has a "head" or nucleus somewhere and extends tentacles of influence from that.

3. It is possible that the nucleus is somewhere in Antarctica.

4. For some reason, people in a waking state are not susceptible to the parasite. It is when conscious control is absent that the Dream Eater can attack.

5. It seems that an early symptom is disturbed sleep and a sensation of being trapped in a nightmare. The warning suggests that the Dream Eater uses fear to weaken its prey.

6. When it has absorbed all life on earth, the Dream Eater will fracture into multiples of itself and infest the universe in search of other planets with life.

7. In some way the meteorite held or paralyzed the Dream Eater's energy and may possibly be a tool of control.

At this time, "Gemini" is unable to advance any theory on:

1. The identity and role of the "Bright Star" child who is supposed to be born at the end of the year 1986 to one of rare beauty.

2. The identity and role of the twins who are supposed to prepare the way for the child.

3. How the child will be able to destroy the Dream Eater.

Starbright put the pages down on the envelope beside her. A breeze like a small sigh disturbed them, and she rested her hand on them to prevent them from falling into the river. The sun was now low at her back, and in front of her, long shadows pointed toward the horizon. Trees, fences, cattle, golden with light, were all joined to strips of dark night. Where willow shadows lay across the river, the burning water ceased and became a deep hole of nothingness. Starbright rested her eyes on the contrast. You can't have sunshine without shadows, Poppa was fond of saying. She looked down at the page under her hand. Her fingers, resting on the paper, made prison bars of shadow. She saw two words in a gap: Bright Star. Star Bright. Then her eyes picked up "rare beauty." Those were the exact words Mumma and Poppa used when they talked about Esther to other people.

They didn't say handicapped. They said rare beauty and specially gifted, which was true as true.

June 5, 1986: New York

"Gemini" has lunch with his sister, who is a retired obstetrics nurse now in public-health nursing. She tells him she is tired of city pressure and is moving to a rural community. She has accepted a job with an agency, doing postoperative nursing for elderly persons. Her territory will cover several small towns and farming areas. As she talks, he realizes that his twin sister and he himself are the twins of the prophecy. He is greatly excited by the discovery, although his sister reacts with scorn. She laughs when he tells her that she will assist in the birth of the Bright Star on the night of December 6.

December 6, 1986

The second prediction of arrival has been fulfilled. The Bright Star is born exactly when and where predicted and "Gemini's" sister assists in the delivery. The twins decide to keep the location a secret lest publicity impede the child's destiny.

Starbright hugged her knees so hard her bones creaked. Then she laughed. Hoo-diddly! The author of the article was related to the Tietz woman. Gemini! Twins!

She had to admit that the article had got to her. It wasn't exciting like a book or film, but it had sucked her into it, all the same. December 6, 1986, was the birthdate of about ten thousand people. More than that. How many billion people on earth? How many days in the year? She leaned over the edge of the bridge to watch a couple of monarch butterflies tumbling around each other in the fading light. Lots of bugs by the river this summer, brown-backed beetles, helicopter dragonflies, ladybugs, spiders on their own bungee cords, all food for the Dream Eater when it had run out of people and cows and sparrows. Wow! Real *X-Files* stuff! She laughed what Poppa called her fat chuckle, and then she remembered the woman who had given her the envelope. The chuckle faded into a frown. Not everyone came back to the real world. Kids at school read newspapers with headlines like "I Was Married to a Vampire" or "Baby Born with Angel Wings" and honestly swallowed incredible garbage like it was the Declaration of Independence. Why were they so gullible? She flicked back through the pages she had just read and had to admit that there was something inside her, the lion feeling again, that wanted to think the Dream Eater was true. It was exactly as Mrs. Okay Keppler had said: Human beings were born with too much imagination.

At the back of the article were more copies of photos, most of them blurred, more graphs, some maps and a heap of English translations from Spanish newspapers. The language was mostly boring, and if there was one thing that turned Starbright off, it was words that sat on the page like concrete pancakes. She loved words with color, words with bounce, words that slipped around her mouth like sherbet or watermelon seeds, and if she couldn't find words like that, well, she just made up her own.

The last page was blank except for a small smudgy photograph of a bearded man and some writing that went diagonally across the page like a spider's walk. "Gemini is my twin brother, Jacob Tietz. Lena Tietz."

That was all.

She stuffed the papers back in the envelope. Then, with the envelope tucked under her T-shirt, she played her usual game of dare with the old bridge, hopping over the gaps where the timbers had fallen away. As usual, she won.

"Nah!" she said as she ran through the hay stubble along the riverbank. "Nah!" as her foot broke the top crust of a cow pie. She stopped to wipe off the green ooze that clogged her sandals and foot. Hoo-diddly! That meteorite business was just like all those people who swore on their mother's grave that a flying saucer had landed in their yard. And right now, if she picked up some flower seeds between her toes, she would have a flumshous foot garden blooming by the time she got home. Yay, those Coulter cows stank!

As she pushed under the hedge between the farm and the road, the envelope fell out from under her T-shirt. She shoved it back, wanting to keep it from her family but not knowing why.

Believe it, said the lion inside.

She hesitated for a second and then laughed. "Nah!" she shouted down the road.

CHAPTER SEVEN

"Starbright Connor, you wash your feet this instant, and not in the house. The garden faucet."

"Yes, Mumma."

"We had this talk before about you running cross-country barefooted."

"I had my sandals on, Mumma."

"Flimsy sandals, next-to-nothing sandals! What about your shoes?"

"Too tight, Mumma. They grinch my feet."

"Grinch! What kind of word is that? Talk sense, child, and scrub good between those toes before you go in to help your sister. I can't leave you one hour without your getting up to something. Hurry, now."

"Sure, Mumma. Be there in two winkles."

Mumma flew back into the kitchen, slamming the screen door. She wasn't cross about anything in particular. Mumma was like an engine, revs getting louder the faster she went, and she sure was busy tonight, late home from the dress fitting because she and Mrs. Morse had been talking. She banged the cooking things too, pots *ding-dong*ing on the faucets, silverware clanking in the drawer. Starbright turned on the faucet outside the kitchen and stuck her green foot under it. You could always tell how late Mumma was by the amount of hurry noise she made.

Before Starbright had half cleaned her toes, the sounds from the kitchen were swallowed up by the music next door, Mark at his trumpet practice. Notes ran up and down and over the fence, as bright as sunlight. They came out so clear and bold, it was like Mark was saying to the neighborhood, Listen man, this is my real voice.

She straightened up to look across the fence, and the envelope under her T-shirt fell out, plop, into the puddle under the faucet. Oh darn! She shook the paper and clamped it back under her shirt not two seconds before Poppa's pickup came whootling down the drive.

"Hi, Poppa!"

"What's that?" he bellowed out the truck window.

"Nothing. Just saying hi." She folded her arms against the envelope.

"Sorry, girl. Can't hear you! Blows a mean horn, our Mark. Mumma and Esther in? I've got a surprise, here, big apple cake, smells like it was made in heaven. I remembered apple cake is one thing our Mark really likes. You want to invite him over for dessert? Tell him to leave his trumpet at home." He climbed out of the truck, thin as a fold-up ruler, balancing a large cake box on his open hand. He quick eyed the faucet, the puddle, and grinned. "Mumma send you outside to wash your feet? Must be bad."

"Cow pie, Poppa."

"What'd you say? Can't hear a word. Never mind. You go tell Mark we got some apple cake tastes better than that trumpet."

They ate dessert on the back porch, Mumma and Poppa sitting on the swing, Esther in the rocker and Mark and Starbright on the step. It was good cake, sure enough, slices of apple dusted with cinnamon and sugar on a sweet dough with a crunch of almonds on top. Pushkin, the cat, was trying to get his nose into Esther's dish, and she was letting him do it.

Poppa had been talking about the Chilean wine

thing, and Mumma was saying, "Maybe now every-one'll stop being so preoccupied with their dreams. I'm sick and tired of hearing dream talk, people worried if they dream and worried more if they don't." She looked at Poppa. "All right, I do it my-self, honey. It's not knowing is the problem. Now they've found the virus in the wine—"

"They haven't yet," said Poppa. "But they're sure they will find it. Chilean wine, the Zimmer-mans. It can't be coincidence, you understand."

Starbright hugged the front of her T-shirt although the envelope was now in her bedroom, tucked under the mattress. "It must be the wine," she said.

"Esther new dress," Esther told Mark. She rocked in her chair. "Red dress. Beautiful dress. Beautiful red church dress."

Starbright turned. "Esther, you already told Mark that a zillion times."

"Sorry," Esther laughed. "Sorry, sorry. Sorry, Mark, sorry, Starbright baby."

"I am not a baby!" There were times when Starbright could not conceal her irritation with the way Esther repeated things. Not that speaking her mind made any difference. She'd just get a glare from Poppa followed by a lecture from Mumma about Esther's birth and how the head injuries caused a problem with language. Esther was a whiz with music and art, and people said she had a healing touch. But she couldn't read or write, and she had to keep hammering at words to pin them down to meaning. Starbright knew all that, but it didn't stop her from getting scritchy with Esther. She ignored Mumma's look and added, "I really hate you calling me baby."

"Sorry, baby," said Esther. "Sorry, sorry—"

"Sister," said Mumma.

"Sister, sister, sorry, sister, sorry, sorry, sister—"

"That's all right, sweetheart," said Poppa.

Mark said, "The dress must be nice, Esther. Bet you're pleased. A new red dress to wear to church. You go to the Unitarian church by the park, don't you? Mrs. Keppler from school goes there, too. You know her?" He looked from Esther to Mumma and then down at his plate. "Mrs. Connor, how come you got an Irish name, eat Jewish desserts and go to the Unitarian church?"

Poppa put his arm around Mumma, and they smiled at each other. This was one more story that Starbright had heard many times over.

"Judy and I met at college," Poppa said to Mark.

"I was Catholic and she was Jewish, and our families didn't want us to marry, but well, we did anyway and then we didn't know where to place our faith. So guess what we did. We sat down with a pen and paper and worked out all the beliefs our religions had in common. Then we looked around for a community of worshippers that fitted the list. We decided on the Unitarian church."

Mark said, "How did your families feel about that?"

"They probably don't know," said Mumma. "Apart from cards at Hanukkah and Christmas, we're a bit out of touch. Simon's parents moved back to Ireland. My father died, and my mother lives in California."

Starbright put her plate down on the step and turned to Mumma. "Were any of them around when I was born?"

"Who?" said Mumma.

"Grandparents."

Mumma looked at Starbright for the longest time, then said, "No, of course not. What put that idea in your head?"

She shrugged. "Just wondered."

"Why do you wonder?" Mumma insisted. "You know. I've told you a dozen times or more—"

"Hoo-diddly, Mumma! It was only a little question. You know, it's kind of weird growing up with a bunch of old photographs as a substitute for grandparents and uncles and aunts and cousins. Mark's got cousins who come and visit. He's got his uncle Ned and auntie Rhoda."

"Yeah, yeah." Mark was getting embarrassed. He stood up. "Great apple cake," he said to Mumma and Poppa. "It was seriously, fantastically delicious, and I can't believe I had three helpings. Thanks for inviting me."

"Bug lights!" cried Esther, pointing to some fireflies that had appeared under the plum tree. "Look, look! Beautiful bug lights!"

"You don't have to go!" Starbright said to Mark.

"I've got homework," he said.

She wanted to show him the stuff in the envelope. She wanted to tell him about the crazy woman who was like a character invented in a story. "I'll come over soon as I've finished the dishes," she said. "I'll help with your homework."

"Bug lights, bug lights!" said Esther, jiggling in her chair.

"It's music homework." Mark was in one of his don't-you-crowd-me moods. "I'm really, really tired, Starbright."

"All right, I'll come over in the morning, then. We'll walk to school."

He hesitated and she thought he was going to say no, but he shrugged an okay and strolled toward the gate in the wooden fence. Esther jumped up and ran after him, hugging his arm, laughing, pointing out the fireflies. Starbright noted that he didn't look too tired as he laughed back. Hoo-diddly! He always liked Esther. That kind of pleased her. She wanted her friends to like Esther. It made her day when Jazzy said Esther was the closest thing to being an angel that people ever got in this world. But sometimes, like now, Mark just plain overdid the liking. He let Esther drag him over to the plum tree and then, clean forgetting his tiredness, he copied her bug-light dance, waving his arms up and down and laughing something stupid. Mumma and Poppa sat in the swing, arms around each other, nodding as though it was completely normal for people to pretend to be fireflies.

Starbright got up and clattered the empty dishes together. She slammed the porch screen door and went in to load the dishwasher. Sure enough, Esther came in running, having picked up the waves of unhappiness from as far away as the plum tree. How did she always know what Starbright was feeling?

"Poor baby, poor baby."

Starbright rested her head on Esther's shoulder and let herself be hugged. She let Esther stroke her hair and cheek with a slow touch, and she felt the gentleness sink into her flesh and blood and bones.

"Poor baby, poor bright star baby."

Starbright drew back a little. "Esther, why do you call me bright star?"

Esther laughed. "Bright star, Starbright, Esther. Bright star, Starbright, Esther." She was counting on her fingers. "Bright star, Starbright, Esther, bright star, Starbright, Esther . . ." She was making a game of it.

Starbright had the words fixed in her head. *There will be born of rare human beauty a child without fear, known as the Bright Star.* Something flicked through her like a fast flame. She laughed. Nah. Course not. Anyway, she felt fear. Sure, she did. She was afraid that Mark would forget and take the bus in the morning instead of waiting for her. She was afraid that she had ruined her white leather sandals with cow dung. Right now, she was afraid she had turned on the dishwasher without detergent.

She looked at Esther, who was chanting a finger

count of their names. "Esther, do you remember when I was born?"

There, she had said it right out loud. She waited for something to happen, but there was no change in Esther's face. Her eyes shone like always, and like always, it was impossible to get past the shining to what Esther was thinking.

"Beautiful sister baby," Esther said.

"Sister hocklepush!" laughed Starbright, hugging her. "I know what you are. You're my guardian angel."

She showered and brushed her teeth, and then, with her mouth awash with peppermint and her skin smelling faintly of roses, she stretched out in her bed with a deep sigh of contentment. Her bed, sure enough, was a magic book, and every night it brought her a new story that was somewhere between truth and fiction. At best, her dreams were exciting adventures; at worst, they were a repeat of an ordinary day, but they were never scary. That was because she was in control of what went on in her own head.

She had tried to explain this to her friends. Hoodiddly! Dreams were just freewheeling thoughts, and thoughts could be steered, even if you were asleep.

In Starbright's sleep, there was always a point of wakefulness that said: This is my dream. I can do what I like with it. Which she did. Sometimes a dream was slow, she decided, just a flumsy floating of everyday things, and sometimes it skitterwhizzed like a roller-coaster with her on board directing it with both hands. If she didn't like a dream, she could walk away from it or change it, tear it up like a messed-up page in her writing book. The thing was, everyone owned their dreams. Why couldn't Mark and Jazzy understand that?

She closed her eyes and sighed.

Most dreams were a mixture of feelings and experience, and it wasn't difficult to work out where they came from. Even as she drifted into an image of dark space, she recognized the *True Sightings* article at work. Why, hoo-diddly, she had that envelope sitting under the mattress like a cow pie, fertilizing the images that ran like a movie through her head.

The darkness of space went on forever, but she was huge in it, standing with her arms and legs outstretched, fingers, eyes, hair, all cold as steel in a rushing wind. With the wind came layers of cloud, black, purple, dark green, running fast as rivers, and in the cloud flickers of lightning. She leaned forward.

Yes, she knew the lightning. She had been waiting for it. It cracked whips of fire all around her and had a chemical smell like burned-up sugar and some kind of ointment, a tarry sweetness that caught in the back of her throat. As she stood there, the smell grew stronger, making her wheeze and cough.

Her control mechanism kicked in. She reached out to grab the lightning like a handful of spaghetti and was surprised when it retreated from her, hissing and flickering. She stepped forward through a drift of dark cloud and once more grabbed at it. This time it disappeared through a hole like an army of electric snakes, and the wind blew hard again, tearing the cloud to shreds and tossing it about so that she was unable to see beyond her hands. The burned-sugar smell was still with her.

Time to dump this dream, she thought, and she turned away, deliberately placing herself in a park-like garden of lawn and trees and trellised roses. In the middle of the garden was an open circular building made of white marble, white steps to a white floor, white columns supporting a domed roof, white table in the middle. As she walked closer, the building touched her with a cold breath, and she realized that it was constructed entirely of ice. She put her hand on a fluted column and felt the deep chill of it. The wind came up and blew a shower of white rose petals over her, like snowflakes. She brushed them off and walked to the picnic table, which had now turned into a slab of white ice. There was something dark in the slab, something that was trying to move. As she came near, a hand reached out through the ice, fingers curled toward her. It was a man's hand, pale but ordinary, with bluish-white nails and dark hair growing on the knuckles. She touched it. It was freezing cold. But the contact made the hand turn and try to grab her fingers. She pulled away and saw, close to the surface of the ice, a face to match the hand. The skin was of the same blue pallor, and there was curly hair and a beard more gray than dark, and light-brown eyes. She thought she knew the eyes but could not see them clearly for the ice set over them. She gave her dream power to crack the ice, and as it fell in splinters away from the lips, she saw the mouth moving. "Bright star," it whispered. "The overlay."

"The what?" She leaned forward.

The pale lips struggled to move in their frame of frost. "The overlay," they repeated.

The sound was drowned in a great roaring as the wind rushed in between her and the block of ice. Before she could think, the building changed to an iceberg and she was standing on it, floating in a frozen wilderness of pack ice and dark sea. The slab in front of her had grown, but she could still make out the dark shape of the man inside, set like a fly in amber. She frowned, pushing all the power of her thinking into smashing the ice. This time, nothing happened. Crooked lines of lightning danced across the sky, and the pack ice growled around her feet. The man shape in the iceberg grew smaller, fainter, then disappeared.

On top of the great white slab, a book blew in the wind, its pages crackling like flags. The book was too high for her to see detail, but she knew that it was important. She stood on her toes and floated up past the wall of ice to the top of the berg, then came down lightly in front of the book, which was now closed and as large as a table. She needed both hands to lift back the cover. There were no words, just pictures. The first was a photo of the man in the ice. His eyes were closed, his face and beard a pale smudge under the glassy surface. She wanted to say that he was sleeping, but she knew that he was dead. On the next page, she saw her friend Jasmine, and although she was not covered with ice, her eyes were also closed. Jazzy's skin, normally the rich color of chestnuts, was a washed-out gray, and her hair, braided with Moroccan money beads, looked oddly dark against her gray scalp.

Starbright turned the photo over and saw Drew next, then Marta and Marilyn and Mrs. Keppler with her eyes sunk in and her mouth slack.

This dream is getting too weird, Starbright thought. What is needed here is a little more control.

She waited, gathering strength while chunks of ice fell from the iceberg into a sea as dark as the sky. The next photograph, she told herself aloud, will show ducks swimming on the Stanton River.

The next photo was of Mark lying in a coffin.

She wondered, then, if she should finish the dream and wake up, but something told her she had to look at the rest of the book. Miss Tietz, the nurse woman, was next, then other kids from school, including Dan Coulter, who looked a lot smaller with his eyes shut and his mouth hanging open.

Okay, Starbright, okay, okay, you know this is just a dream.

Mumma was there and so was Poppa. She turned the page and saw a picture of herself, Starbright Connor, lying in her pajamas on a block of ice like some fish in a shop window. She studied the shadows under her eyes, the sharpness of her nose and cheekbones. She held the corner of the next page for a long time, unwilling to turn to the last photograph. Finally, she did it, and yes, the book ended with Esther. Her sister was wearing her red dress and her eyes were not closed. They were wide and empty, the shining replaced by a dull film.

That did it. Instantly, Starbright changed. She did not even have to think about dream control. One moment she was looking at the picture of Esther, the next she was a furious lion with a pelt as dark as wild honey and long claws that slashed blue and green crevasses in the ice. The roar that had been growing in her burst from her jaws as a great rolling flame. Nothing could stop it. She was like an erupting volcano. Under the fire of her breath, the book of the dead lit up for an instant. Then it turned to a pale-gray ash that washed away in a stream of melting ice. Still the roar went on, sending the wind back on its course, boiling the dark sea—

"Starbright! Starbright!"

The lion closed its mouth on the taste of burned sugar.

"Wake up, Starbright."

"Huh?"

"It's all right, Starbright. You're only dreaming."

The light was on. They were both there, Mumma and Poppa leaning over her, Mumma shaking her arm, looking scared. The quilt had fallen off the bed, and the sheet was wound tight around her feet.

"You okay, girl?" Poppa said.

She sat up and scratched the back of her neck.

Mumma sat on the edge of the bed and felt Starbright's forehead. "I couldn't believe the noise you were making. It was bad, wasn't it?"

Starbright nodded, then yawned and lay down. "I'm okay, Mumma."

"You never have bad dreams," said Mumma.

"Let's fix up this bed," said Poppa, trying to straighten the sheet.

"We thought someone was trying to murder you," Mumma said, picking up the quilt. "Oh, sweetheart, do you still feel frightened?"

"I wasn't frightened," said Starbright. "I was angry."

Mumma looked at Poppa. "It's this Claircomb business, Simon. I'm sick of it! Everyone's an expert at scaremongering! It's got so sensible people are dreaming themselves into nervous breakdowns."

"Oh, I wouldn't say that," Poppa replied. "All of us get the occasional nightmare. Stick your feet in, girl. Do you want a thicker pillow?"

"No thanks, Poppa."

"Poor baby. Poor, poor baby." Esther was standing in the doorway, twisting a strand of dark-red hair against the shoulder of her nightgown.

"I wasn't screaming," said Starbright. "I was yelling because I was good and mad."

"Mad at what?" said Mumma.

"We'll talk about it in the morning," Poppa said, steering Mumma away. "Go back to bed, Esther. Your sister was dreaming, you understand. Nothing to worry about."

Starbright bunched the pillow around her face. "Did I really make such a galumping noise?" she asked.

"Believe me," said Poppa. "Enough to waken the dead."

By morning she had it all worked out. When she had read the magazine article yesterday, she had told herself that it would make a good horror movie. So that was what her mind did with it. Cheap film, huh? The actor with the beard would have been the woman's twin brother, Jacob Tietz.

His face had been blurred in the smudged photo-copy of the article.

Getting mad when she saw the picture of Esther related to the other day at school, when she got fussled over slopmouth Dan Coulter. You didn't need a degree in dreamology to work that out.

The smell of burned sugar puzzled her. Usually, dreams didn't have smells. But that mystery cleared when she pushed through the gate in the fence, to see if Mark was ready to leave for school.

"Mrs. Dudnelly? Is Mark about?"

"Mark isn't going to school today, Starbright." Mrs. Dudnelly patted her orange hair. "I am not at all surprised. He told me last night he had three helpings of sweet apple cake."

"He's sick?" Starbright asked.

"It's not your fault," Mrs. Dudnelly said. "No one is blaming you, Starbright. Mark knows full well there are some things pure poison to him. He's not diabetic exactly. It's just he simply cannot toler-ate a scrap of sugar. Have you any idea what sugar does to people?"

Starbright did have an idea. Mark was always talking about it. Sugar was called the white death, he said.

Sugar smell. White marble. White ice. White

death. Hoo-diddly! Weren't dreams amazing things?

She had a grin as wide as a watermelon slice when she said, "I'm sure sorry, Mrs. Dudnelly."

The woman nodded. "When Mark wakes up, I'll tell him you called."

The envelope stayed with Starbright all day. Her best friends, Mark and Jazzy, were not at school, and some of the others kids, including Marilyn, were away with the gymnastics team in Bannerville. That left Drew, and he was so wrapped up in space comics and UFO stuff, she couldn't tell him about the magazine article. What about Mrs. Keppler? Their teacher knew about the signals in Argentina, and she would be able to tell Starbright that it was all a lot of flimmy rotdust. But Mrs. Okay Keppler was not okay. She was in a scritchy mood, no time for a smile even, so the yellow envelope didn't come out of Starbright's backpack until school was out. Then she held it under her arm and looked along the line of cars for the nurse woman Lena Tietz, and yes, she was right there, wearing dark glasses, waving and getting out of her little green car so fast, you'd think it was on fire, and hoo-diddly, would you believe it, parked three cars in front was the truck with Poppa and Esther in it.

Quick as a blink, Starbright passed the envelope to the woman and said, "I'm sorry. I can't stay. My sister and my father are waiting for me."

"You read it?"

She saw the truck door opening. "Most of it. I have to go."

"Starbright, this is urgent." The woman held her arm. "We must talk about it. Can we meet at the Bella Vista Café? I'm staying at the motel next door."

"No!" Starbright stepped back. "I'm really sorry. I don't believe in this kind of stuff."

"That's all right! It's what I said to my brother. He said believing didn't matter. If you're part of it, it will happen anyway. But now there isn't much time. It's going to move very quickly."

Starbright tried to sidestep, but the woman moved in front of her.

Lena Tietz waved the envelope. "I need to instruct you! I'm the only one left!"

Esther was out of the truck and coming toward them with quick bouncing steps, her arms held out wide like her smile.

"No!" Starbright jumped away from the woman. "I mean no! I don't want anything to do—"

"You are the overlay!" the woman cried.

The word hit Starbright's ear as sharp as a stone and she stopped, her mouth open. She tested the echo in her head and repeated, "Overlay?"

Lena Tietz took off her glasses. Her eyes were red and swollen. "That was my brother's description of the second path. You read about the second path in his notes?"

There was no time to answer, because now Esther was upon them, bouncing in her paint-spattered shirt and shorts. Her laughter was shrill with surprise, and her arms, which had been out-stretched toward Starbright, suddenly turned and closed around Miss Tietz. "Baby lady!" Esther shouted.

The envelope and sunglasses flew out of Miss Tietz's hands and she stood there, awkwardly patting Esther on the back. Esther went on hugging the woman and laughing fit to bust. "Baby lady! Push, push, that's my big star!"

Poppa came out of the truck, running.

"It's good to see you again, Esther," said Miss Tietz.

"Esther!" Poppa called. "Sweetheart?"

Esther let go of the woman but didn't look toward Poppa. She grabbed Starbright by the shoulders and turned her all the way around to show her front and back and front again to the woman, and then she said, her eyes shining like car lights, "Look! Look! Esther's beautiful baby!"

CHAPTER EIGHT

Mumma said to Starbright, "We thought the nurse had told you."

"She didn't," said Starbright, sitting on Poppa's side of the bed. This was the place of personal talks, the front room with the lace curtains that sucked in and out of the window and Mumma's Exercycle used for draping damp laundry, and the oak dressing table with the smooching photo of Mumma and Poppa just married. Mumma half sat, half lay on her part of the bed. "It wasn't a lie," she said. "We did adopt you. Legally, we are your parents and Esther is your sister, and that's how it's been for twelve years."

"The other day the nurse let slip something about it," said Starbright. "Something about my grandparents. Then she said she was sorry, she'd made a mistake. You should have told me, Mumma."

"Darling, we were honestly going to tell you,"

said Mumma. "Sooner or later you'd see your birth certificate or you'd meet someone who knew us in those days. But we thought if we could wait a few years—"

"I wish you'd said," Starbright insisted. She picked at a loose thread on the bedspread.

"Well, you know now," said Mumma. "But it wasn't the way we wanted you to find out. I am sorry about that."

"Hoo-diddly, Mumma! I already told you I'm pleased. Now things make sense."

"What things, honey?"

"Like the way Esther always calls me baby. Like the way you never, never talk about how I was born. It's always what happened when Esther was born."

"Oh, sweetheart, that's because she nearly died."

"Yeah, well, I used to think her head injuries made her birth more important than mine, and I wished something had happened to me, too, so you would talk about when I was a baby."

"Oh, Starbright! Oh, my little lamb!" Mumma put her arm around her. "Why didn't you say something?"

Starbright shrugged and twisted the thread around her finger. The bedspread puckered.

"I'm not making any big wallabazoo about it. Things don't have to change. I mean, it's okay with me if I go on calling Esther my sister, and you'll still be Mumma and Poppa. I just want to tell you that knowing makes a difference. I wish I'd always known."

Mumma let her hand fall warm on Starbright's arm. "Poppa and I talked it over more times than we can count. Our big worry was we didn't have a scrap of information about your natural father."

Natural father? Starbright sat up straight. Her world with Mumma, Poppa and Esther was so complete that she had not considered anyone else. But everyone had a father, and there was someone out there who was half of her. She thought awhile about that but, apart from surprise, felt nothing.

"Who is he?" she asked.

"We haven't the faintest idea," said Mumma. "When Esther was fourteen and a half, she went to a camp for the disabled. She was away for two weeks. When she came home, she was happy as always. Did you ever know Esther when she wasn't happy? Then she started putting on weight. She couldn't do up her jeans, and her bras were too tight. When our doctor told us she was pregnant, we couldn't believe it. We had more tests done."

"Didn't she say anything?"

"No. She talked about swimming at the camp and the horses and the food. Poppa and I didn't want to go too far with our questions. We felt either she didn't understand what had happened or else she forgot. Esther has always been so loving and trusting. We had to be very careful we didn't damage that. She loved to joke about her fat tummy. She was very proud of it, but she didn't seem to know there was a baby inside. It was as though she wasn't making any connections between what happened at camp, her big tummy and your arrival. Well, that's what we thought."

"What about you and Poppa?" Starbright asked, not looking up. "How did you feel when you found she was pregnant?"

Mumma laughed. "At first we were surprised. Amazed, I should say. And worried of course. All those questions of who, where and how. Then we got past that and we were so happy, we couldn't stop celebrating. You were a miracle, Starbright. The doctors said I couldn't have any more babies, and we knew that Esther would never marry. We thought we were the end of the line."

"You were pleased, then." Starbright broke the thread and flattened the bedspread.

"Pleased? Pleased?" Mumma shook her head. "The greatest word inventor in the world can only think of *pleased?*"

"Very pleased," said Starbright. "Hoozled. Wanged out of your thinking tree."

"Closer," said Mumma. "You know the crystal vase with the seam of glue? Got knocked over when Poppa tried to dance on the table with a wine glass on his head. He didn't spill the wine. Just kicked the vase against the wall. We were so happy, Starbright, every day was a song to dance to. Believe it. Sure we had questions, but the answers didn't seem nearly as important as you and Esther. Honey, having you was the best thing to happen to us."

"Really hoozled," said Starbright. "Big-time wanged." She crawled on her elbows to Mumma's side of the bed. "Tell me about it, Mumma."

"Oh yes, yes. We thought a hospital could be strange for Esther. A home birth in her own bedroom with a doctor and midwife. That's what we decided. And such a good doctor we chose, a general practitioner with high qualifications in obstetrics. There would be no problems, he said. Esther had an excellent pelvis, not like me, and the baby was in the right position. We were so excited with the waiting! Then it happened."

"What?"

"You happened. Our little Starbright, who always does things her own way, happened. You came two weeks too early. Not only that. The morning Esther went into labor, the doctor ran off the road in his car and broke his arm. More than that. The midwife was with another patient on the other side of town. You would not wait even for her. The agency had to send a nurse we had never seen before."

"Lena Tietz," said Starbright.

"Oh, we didn't have to worry. She was very good with Esther. So kind. And she knew what she was doing, too. You came into the world with not the tiniest problem. You were perfect. Esther was wonderful. Your poppa and I cried and cried floods but you didn't make a sound, just looked around, waving at us. Miss Tietz said some babies were like that."

"What else did she say, Mumma?"

"I don't remember. We saw her only that night, because the next day the midwife was back and then the doctor came to examine you and Esther was insisting that we call you Starbright instead of Rose." Mumma's smile faded and she frowned.

"Twelve years, and now she turns up on our door-step. We didn't recognize her. Poppa thought she was someone on an errand from the dressmaker."

"What did she say?" asked Starbright.

"Wanted to see you. Wanted to talk to us." Mumma shook her head. "Sweetheart, when you were born, she was fine. We couldn't have gotten better care. I don't know what's happened since then, but that poor woman, she's not herself, and that's putting it mildly. Eyes were jumping clean out from beneath her glasses. I don't want you talking to her, Starbright. You understand that clearly, don't you? Poppa and I decided that none of us should have anything to do with her. I'm sorry to say Miss Tietz is as crazy as a two-dollar watch."

Starbright nodded. That suited her fine. But the story of how she had been born had brought up things that fitted into the woman's craziness in a way that could not be explained, and resting on it all was the word overlay.

Bright Star. . . . The overlay, the man in the ice had said.

How did that get into her dream? What did it mean?

* * *

Esther was in the dining room, painting pictures of dead bugs. Starbright sat on the other side of the table, watching Esther's face focused and smiling over the blobs of color. Sure, Esther had different ways of doing things that sometimes got on her nerves, but they were all happy ways if people weren't in a hurry to appreciate them. Starbright was always in too much of a hoozling hurry. She was first to admit it. It was good to sit still for a change, look at the painting and think about growing in Esther's belly.

"I love this painting," Starbright said, picking up one of the butterfly pictures.

"Lovesee," said Esther. "Beautiful lovesee, baby."

"What's a lovesee?" said Starbright. "Butterfly?"

Esther laughed and laughed, then put her hand over her mouth, wiping fluorescent green paint across her chin. "No, baby, not butterfly. Lovesee. Baby lovesee."

Starbright laughed too, although she didn't know what the joke was. "Inventing words is hereditary," she said. She wanted to add "Mom" but didn't.

"Look, look!" Esther got out of her chair, took the butterfly picture and held it against Starbright's face so close the colors blurred. "Beautiful lovesee! Baby lovesee. Got it, bright star baby?"

"Sure, Esther. Got it," Starbright said, not getting it at all, and Esther sat down again. She picked up her paintbrush, put her tongue firmly at the corner of her green-spattered mouth and filled in the wings of another butterfly with bright purple.

In the bug collection on the table, there was a dead monarch butterfly Esther had found in the garden shed, faded orange wings closed, one antenna missing. She was painting it the way a kindergarten child paints butterflies, thick body, bright-colored wings edged in black. Esther's butterflies weren't monarchs, they weren't orange, they weren't dead. They flip-flapped across the paper as though they were trying to escape, bright fat things that could maybe turn into birds or tropical fish or kites in a windstorm. But Esther, sure as jumbly, thought she was doing photographic paintings of monarchs.

With her finger, Starbright separated the bug collection, which was mostly an assortment of dried-up beetles and flies that Esther had found on window ledges and in spiderwebs. They were getting old and losing legs and wings.

"Want some more?" Starbright said. "There

are heaps by the river. I can get you a big green-and-blue dragonfly."

Esther stopped painting and sat very still, her head down.

"Not a live one, Esther," said Starbright. "One that's dead already. Promise."

Esther nodded and rinsed her brush in the water jar.

"I can get you feathers, too. Quail, duck, California geese. Do you want some more feathers? Yikes! What's this? Esther, you've got a cockroach here!" Starbright leaned over the long brown body. "A gungeous cockroach!"

"Under piano," said Esther. "Bug under, under. Piano bug."

"It's not a bug. It's a cockroach!"

"Cockroach, cockroach." Esther smiled. "Cockroach, baby. Cockroach." She opened her painting pad and showed Starbright a page full of brown things with legs.

"They're filthy, Esther. Gross! What do you want to paint cockroaches for?"

"No!" Smiling, Esther shook her head. "Beautiful bug. Look!" She picked up the dead cockroach, held it in the palm of her hand and stroked it. "Beautiful lovesee."

"No, Esther." Starbright stepped back. "That's not beautiful. It's a cockroach. It's pukelagenous. You let Mumma see you've been painting cockroaches on the dining-room table and she'll squeech like a fire siren. Put it away."

Esther's smile wobbled a bit as she put the cockroach into her pencil box and closed the lid. Starbright imagined that she could hear the thing crunch. She said, "Sorry, Esther. Cockroaches are definitely not nice. They carry disease."

"Now dragonfly bug," said Esther. "Now Starbright dragonfly bug, now baby, now baby, now—"

"Later," said Starbright. "I'm going next door to see Mark. When I come back, we'll go down to the river and look for feathers and dragonflies. Okay?"

"Okay, okay!" Esther's smile grew huge and she slapped the table, making her brushes bounce and rattle. Then she jumped up to put her arms around Starbright.

Although Starbright wanted to get the word Mom out just once, it would not come. What she said was "I love you, Esther!"

"Beautiful baby!" said Esther, almost squeezing the breath out of her. She suddenly let go and snatched up one of the butterfly paintings. "For

Mark. Monarch bug for Mark. Go Mark, baby, picture bug Mark."

Mark was lying on the couch watching a football game. "I thought you weren't coming."

"I said I would." Starbright sat sideways in an armchair, hanging her legs over the edge. "I got talking to Mumma and then Esther. This is yours. One of Esther's paintings. She wanted you to have it."

"Butterflies." He held the paper above his head. "Her paintings are kind of modern, aren't they?"

"Kind of Esther," she said. She realized that Mark was looking pale as a maggot, with dark smudges under his eyes. "You been throwing up?"

He put down the painting and let his arms hang limp. "No, just sick," he said in a weak voice.

Starbright felt her sympathy curl up like a dead leaf. To her, sick was throwing up. You got it over with and then you went on with life. But Mark, she suspected, actually enjoyed being ill. He found illness interesting. "What do you mean sick?" she demanded.

"Apple cake," he said. "I've got a very low tolerance—"

"Of sugar," she said. "I know that. But what kind of sick? Headache? Stomach cramps? Big toe fell off? What's so whoozy you had to miss a three-page essay for Mrs. Not Okay today?"

He knew what she was trying to do, and he would not be cheered. He said, "Allergies run in our family."

She did not want to hear that, either. Less than a week had passed since she and Mark had last been together at the bridge, but in that time, centuries of stuff had happened, and if she didn't talk about it, she would burst wide open like a melon dropped off a truck. She thought she'd give him the super-jumbo news first. "Guess what I found out today!" she said. "Esther is really my mother."

"Oh," he said. "I know that."

She sat up. "You know?"

"Sure. Jazzy told me."

"You're kidding!" She grabbed the remote control and turned off the TV. "Jasmine Collis told you I was Esther's daughter? Who told her?"

"A lot of people know," said Mark. "I mentioned it to Mom. She'd heard ages ago. We reckoned you knew but you just wanted to tell people . . ." His voice faded, and he ended with a shrug.

"We are supposed to be friends and you didn't ever say anything!"

"I dunno, Starbright. I didn't think about it all that much, to tell the truth."

"So it wasn't important!"

He put his hand over his eyes. "I really do feel sick, Starbright. It's not just the sugar. I think I'm coming down with something." He opened his fingers and peered at her. "Measles or something."

She slapped her hands against the arms of the chair. "When did Jazzy tell you? When? Huh?"

"I don't remember. Oh, shush it, will you, Starbright? Esther acts like your mother. She calls you her baby. So what's the big deal? It's your business." He reached for the remote control and turned the TV back on. "You heard about the Zimmermans, didn't you? Mr. Zimmerman died this afternoon. Mrs. Zimmerman is in critical condition."

Starbright closed her mouth.

"There might be something on the six-o'clock news." He began surfing through the channels. "They haven't found any virus in the wine. They're saying now it's probably a kind of cancer."

"They don't know anything," she said. Then she added, "Why didn't Jazzy tell me she knew?"

"There's a cancer expert," said Mark. "Oncologist whatshisname. He says the stuff that causes the cancer, carcinogens, is in the environment. That's why it breaks out in some places and not others."

Starbright watched the bright patchwork of images on the shifting channels. "Did they say anything about it coming from space—you know, a meteorite or something like that?"

"No." He hesitated on a news bulletin, but it was an item about an earthquake in Iran. "You know what? They think it could be additives in food. Coloring and stuff."

"Everyone eats that. What are you going to do? Give up eating altogether?"

His face was too anxious for joking. She looked away and shrugged. "Good grief, Mark, nobody knows the Zimmermans had spindle sickness. It could have been anything." She thought about her dream, the book of photos and the picture of Mark lying in a coffin. Then she thought of Esther. How come Mark and his mother and just about everyone else had known that Esther was her mother? How come they had not told her?

She swung out of the chair, stomped over to the TV and pulled the plug out of the wall socket. "Don't tell me you've been slummeried on the couch all day watching dismal TV news. No wonder you're sick!"

He threw the remote control on the floor and put his hands behind his head. "Starbright, I got something to tell you. It's not the sugar."

"What?"

"I told Mom it was the sugar but it's not. I think I've got spindle sickness."

"Spindle sickness? Bishbosh!" She made herself laugh.

"I'm scared to go to sleep, Starbright. Honestly, truthfully swear to God, the dreams are so bad my heart hurts—I can't breathe. I really think I could die in my sleep!"

"That's sugar, Mark. You said it made your heart go crazy."

He shook his head. "Not just last night. Every night. It's getting worse. You said anyone can control their dreams. I know I'm dreaming. I say to myself, All I have to do is wake up. But I don't know how to wake up. It won't happen. These guys are hunting me with guns and knives and stuff. I can't get away from them and I can't wake up. Last night I dreamed they killed me."

Starbright leaned forward. "Did you see any lightning in your dream?"

"No."

"Any snow and ice?"

"No. But I saw you. I did. After they shot me. I was dead and everything was dark. Then I heard your voice. You said something about ducks and the Stanton River. I heard you clear as anything. Then suddenly there was bright light and you were leaning over me. You looked surprised, and the wind was blowing your hair. I woke up soon afterward, but I felt terrible. Mom's made an appointment for me to see Dr. Abinado tomorrow morning." He bit at a fingernail.

"Ducks," said Starbright. "Ducks on the Stanton River."

"I know it doesn't make sense. But it was real."

Starbright looked away. She'd been ready to tell him the fantastically entertaining story of the crazy woman and the yellow envelope full of weird stuff. She had wanted to make him laugh with her. Now she caught her breath and held it in silence.

"I can't tell you how scary it is," he said.

He had been there, she thought. In some freakish way, his dream and her dream had run together. She had been on the iceberg, looking at the book of photos. What she had said was "The next photograph will show ducks swimming on the Stanton River," but the next photo had been of Mark lying in a coffin.

She felt shaken to the bone. She had told no one about last night's dream, and yet twice today someone had used words from it. She said to Mark, "Maybe the doctor can give you something to make you sleep without dreaming."

"It won't work. Each night gets worse."

"Bet you anything it was the sugar," she said. "You've got so many allergies. Look, you know that woman your mom saw at the door? The one calling out? She was the nurse when I was born. She knows quite a lot about dreams. I could talk to her, if you like."

He didn't answer.

"Dr. Abinado'll do some tests. Hoo-diddly, you might have diabetes and not know it."

He gave her a long mournful look and then went back to watching the blank TV screen.

She stood up, stretched her arms and smiled as best she could. "Some of the kids were over at Bannerville for the gymnastics meet. You want to go to Marilyn's and find out how they did?"

That made him look at her. "Starbright, don't you ever listen to anything? I've been telling you, I'm sick, sick, sick! I can't go anywhere."

He was telling the truth. He was sick. Her throat ached at the look of him. "I just thought it would flizz you up a bit," she said, trying to hold her smile steady. "Better than lying here imagining you've got spindle sickness."

"I'm not imagining anything," he snapped. "You feel my forehead. Look at my eyes. See how bloodshot they are?"

He dragged down his lower lids, gazing at her like an old bloodhound. His eyeballs were as pink as strawberry ice cream with lines running over them. The bottom lids were red watery cups.

As she looked closer, she caught the warmth of his breath and a familiar smell of something chemical, a bit like burned sugar.

That night, Starbright dreamed again of the windswept space, the dark clouds and the lightning, the smell. In front of her was a large TV screen that showed Mark being hunted by men with guns. Every channel showed the same scene, and although she willed herself to different places—her classroom, a tropical island, a shopping mall— everywhere she went, she saw the same TV screen. In her dream she watched Mark die about twenty times, and she could not do anything about it.

CHAPTER NINE

Lena Tietz was getting music over the phone, the never-ending tinkle of "Greensleeves." She tapped her foot and looked around the motel room—at the brown-and-orange wallpaper, the Japanese print of two carp, the yellow candlewick bedspread with a round cigarette burn, the hard white light at the window cut into strips by the venetian blind.

"Come on, come on!" she snapped at the phone. She was about to hang up when a cheerful young voice came through, "Good morning. Infectious diseases unit, Melbourne Quarantine Hospital."

"Good afternoon. Please put me through to Ward Three." Then she added: "This is an international call. Don't leave me on hold."

"One moment please," the voice chirped.

The head nurse came on immediately, and he did not attempt to paint the world with sunshine. "I am sorry, Miss Tietz," he said. "Your brother's on a monitor and holding his own, but the prognosis is not good. I have your number. I promise you we will phone if there is any change at all. Yes, we know it is an international call. That doesn't matter. We will get in touch with you, Miss Tietz. You have my word." After a slight hesitation, he added. "I believe you are a professional nurse, Miss Tietz."

"Retired," she said.

"You do realize that all victims of spindle sickness are subject to autopsy."

"Yes," she said. "I know."

"That's a government regulation, but I want to tell you that your brother was in full agreement. I am sure he understood that, in donating his body to science, he would be saving the lives of future patients."

"No," said Miss Tietz. "Jacob didn't believe that at all. He knew it wasn't a virus. He told the hospital. He made his research available to you. He gave you factual evidence and you didn't believe a word."

"Miss Tietz, I'm sorry." He spoke gently, slowly. "I understand that Jacob is your only living relative. This must be very painful for you. Do you have someone you can talk to, a grief counsellor—"

She put the phone down and sat there on the bed, shaking, too exhausted for tears. She had no one to talk to. Not a soul. The energy of this invader from space was a force like a flood or an earthquake, and she was a broken matchstick that it had tossed aside. Soon she would join her brother. Oh yes, she knew what was happening. Never had she known such loneliness in dreams, such agonies of fear. Night after night it came, the journey into dark nothingness, the sense of total isolation and the terror of running with no place to go.

The Dream Eater was moving fast.

She had done what she could to instruct the Bright Star and had failed. How did you warn a child who had no fear? Now she had to plan quickly to get to Jacob before he died. She needed to be there beside him, even if she, too, was unconscious. They had been born together. They would die together.

She picked up the phone book and turned to airline toll-free numbers. She would use her credit card to book the first available flight to Melbourne, Australia, and that would be the end of it.

But, with her fingers poised over the phone, she thought again of the baby born in Bannerville twelve and a half years ago. Before she left the country, she must make one last attempt to talk to the Connors. If they still refused to speak to her, then she could leave with a clear conscience. She dialed their number and waited with apprehension. Simon Connor answered. He was very angry. He said that her harassment had become a matter for the police.

"If you call this number again, you will be arrested!" he shouted, and slammed the phone down.

The violence of his anger made her feel sick. She lay back on the bed, her hand over her thudding heart. That's the finish, you stupid man, she thought. I hope you remember this conversation when you see the Dream Eater feeding on your family. I hope that when your own life force is being sucked out of you like the juice from an orange, you will realize that the fate of the world swung the wrong way on your abysmal ignorance.

But Lena Tietz was too tired to continue such thoughts. Melbourne, she muttered to herself. I have to book a plane to Melbourne. Trying to focus clearly, she closed her aching eyes and, almost instantly, fell asleep.

The dream came over her like an inescapable cage, and she choked on her fear as her world became one of emptiness and loss. How could she have closed her eyes? How could she have let it happen again?

She was the only living creature in the entire universe. No, not quite. There was something else there, but she could neither see nor name it. It was a mocking presence that swam in the air. She ran through it to get away from it. She breathed its evil into her gasping lungs and heart. She tried to flee from it in the darkness, but the thing *was* the darkness.

If only there was some way to wake up.

"The motel! The motel!" she called, willing the orange-and-brown room to come to her. She tried to visualize the faded yellow bedspread with its neat brown cigarette burn as she clawed through the menacing darkness, seeking some familiar touch. She found the switch on the lamp beside her bed and pressed it.

Ah! The motel room filled with grainy yellow light and she lay flat on her pillow, gasping with relief. She was awake. Above the bed was the framed Japanese print of carp in a pond, and to the right was the chipped paint of the bathroom door. She held on to these things with her eyes, her heart thudding like a drum. But even as she watched, the bathroom door slid to another wall and the lamp-light, dense as yellow fog, began to shrink from the corners of the room.

"No!" she cried, punching the switch at the base of the lamp, but the light withdrew until it was a faint misty halo around the shade. Then it went out and she was back in darkness. She had not wakened from the dream after all. The motel room had simply become a part of her nightmare.

The feeling of loss and loneliness was an active presence that was trying to overpower her. As weak and breathless as she was, she had to keep running from it. She knew the pattern. The dreams took over until the victims could no longer wake up, and she was getting close to that stage. But she desperately needed to get to her brother. If she could only come out of it one more time, long enough to put herself on a plane.

"Wake up!" Her frantic heart beat out the rhythm. "Wake up, wake up!"

When she opened her eyes to daylight, it was a voice she heard, "Wake up! Wake up, ma'am," and she saw the maid by her bed with an armful of towels. "Excuse me, ma'am, but the rest of the staff have gone home for the day. I have to do this room. Are you okay?"

"Yes," she said. "Oh, yes. Thank you."

"You were sleeping yesterday. You were sleeping this morning and lunchtime and again this afternoon. We wondered maybe you were getting that sickness." The woman put the towels on the bed. "You want to use the bathroom before I clean it?"

Lena Tietz emptied her painfully full bladder and wondered how long she had slept. She felt weak, stiff and very thirsty. She drank two glasses of water and came out of the bathroom thankful, oh so thankful for the floor under the feet, the traffic driving past the window, the solid movements of the maid as she stripped down the bed. "What time is it?"

"Four o'clock, ma'am."

"Saturday afternoon, right?"

The woman gave her a considering look. "Sunday, ma'am."

"Sunday? I've slept more than twenty-four hours?"

"That's right. You missed all the goings-on. The commotion in the streets. Everything. You want to have a shower? Go right ahead. I can come back. I'm not going anyplace."

The last words brought Lena Tietz to a halt. "Melbourne!" she exclaimed. "I need to book a flight to Australia!"

"What for?" said the woman. "You aren't going anyplace either, ma'am. Stanton went under quarantine seven o'clock this morning. Four cases in the hospital yesterday. Maybe more by now. No one can get in the town or out of it unless it's official."

"Spindle sickness?"

"So they say. Three kids and a teacher. You ask me, it's meningitis from that swimming pool. I got a son living down at East Fall Hills, and he can't get home for his birthday on Wednesday. They've all gone mad. You turn on your TV and see what I mean. Roadblocks, miles of yellow tape, National Guard, police, reporters. Lady, you got plenty of time to see it all, 'cause you can forget about any flight to Australia."

"What are the names of the children?"

"I don't recall. One of them plays trumpet in the Stanton brass band. Blows good for a skinny white kid. The teacher's in her forties."

"Is one of the children called Starbright Connor?"

The woman shook her head and flattened the bedcover. "Don't ask me, ma'am. I remember opera. I remember birthdays. I carry colors and figures in my head exact like perfect pitch, but I don't do names. Sorry. You want me to turn on your TV to find out?"

It was not necessary. Before Lena Tietz had a chance to say or do anything, there was a knock and the child was standing in the doorway, rubbing a foot against her ankle. She was wearing shorts and a bleached-out denim shirt, and her black hair, braided over her ears, framed dark eyes in a pale and serious face. "What's an overlay?" she asked.

CHAPTER TEN

Starbright sat in a wood-backed chair and tried not to look too hard at Miss Tietz. The woman was not wearing her glasses, and her eyes were as red as Mark's. Her hands were shaking. So was her voice. The whole room smelled as though someone had cooked sugar and diesel oil together in a frying pan.

"Do your grand— your parents know you are here?"

"They aren't home," Starbright said. "Poppa and Mumma went up to the hospital for tests. They took Esther, but there wasn't room in the truck for me. You heard about Mark and Jazzy?"

"Are they the children in the hospital?"

"And Dan Coulter. And Mrs. Keppler. Tell me about the overlay."

Lena Tietz leaned against the wall, her hand pressed against her forehead. "The overlay is the second path of the prediction. It is much weaker than the main path. No more than a shadow, really. Which is why Jacob coined the word overlay. In the main path, the Dream Eater—" She rubbed her eyes and put on her glasses. "Excuse me. I have quite a headache. I must get an aspirin."

Starbright called to the bathroom after her, "I saw Mark on Friday, and he told me he had spindle sickness. I didn't want to believe him. He can be a bit of a wimpochondriac, you know. But I've been dreaming about him, and I think he's right. It's not ordinary dreaming. It's like—it's like living a movie. I've thought a whole lot about it, and I reckon you and your brother are the only people who know what's going on."

The woman came back and sat in the other chair. "Do you know all the people who are in the hospital with the sickness?"

"Yes."

"I thought so." Lena Tietz sighed. "Starbright, my brother, Jacob, is in a hospital in Australia. He's on life support. He doesn't have long to live."

"He's got it too?"

"Yes."

Starbright thought of the bearded dream man disappearing into the ice. She said, "What about you?"

"The same," said the woman. "I am certain of it. The Dream Eater has grown very strong, Starbright. Now it's powerful enough to remove everything that threatens its survival. When it has accomplished that, the sickness will quickly become a major world epidemic. My brother calculated that it will not take long for the Dream Eater to move over the face of earth, devouring all life. The terrible irony is that Jacob, who has fought it for so long, will soon become part of its energy-devouring evil."

Starbright came back to her original question. "You said I was the overlay," she said.

Miss Tietz put on her glasses. The lenses were badly smudged, but they still enlarged the redness of her eyes. "You read Jacob's article from *True Sightings* magazine? Tell me, how did that make you feel?"

The word *lion* came to Starbright, but she said, "I didn't believe it."

"How do you explain all the coincidences?"

"They could have been made up," said Starbright. "The article was published only a few years ago. You and your brother could have invented the Dream Eater to sell a story."

The woman was not offended. She gave Starbright a tired smile. "We did not invent the

Diaguita message. We did not invent the meteorite. I can show you Jacob's notes written long before your birth. How did we make that up? How did we invent your dreams? How did we manufacture the cycle of spindle sickness around you?"

"Cycle? Around—me?"

"Don't you know what's happening? Starbright, this is what I have been trying to tell you. The Dream Eater is trying to get at you. It works through fear. It must make its victim weak before it can feed from it. We don't understand the reason for that. What we do know, for certain, is that it feeds on our psychic energy, and it does this while we are asleep. All spindle sickness sufferers have nightmares in the early stages of the illness. But the nightmares are all different. It seems that the Dream Eater uses our personal fears to gain access to our energy."

Listening to Lena Tietz speak was not the same as reading the magazine article. The woman's voice connected directly with the restless lion that was roaming about in Starbright's head, and the lion rumbled at every word in a knowing way. Starbright leaned forward. Maybe the story of the Dream Eater was still not *head* real, but sure as spit it was *feeling* real, and it fitted exactly with all the dreams and experiences of the last week.

The woman went on: "In the overlay, the Bright Star, the child without fear, uses the gift that has been given her to overcome the Dream Eater. In the main prediction, the Bright Star fails to use the gift and discovers fear. The Bright Star is then overcome by the Dream Eater. Starbright, this is important. What do you think could cause you fear?"

Starbright was quiet for a moment, then shrugged. "I don't know."

"There must be a weakness. The prediction can't lie. Think hard. Is there any situation that would fill you with terror?"

"I told you—I don't know."

"Then maybe the Dream Eater knows something you don't. What it's doing at the moment is playing a game of chess. You are the threat. You are the king. It is eliminating all the pieces around you to get at you."

"How do you know that?" Starbright asked.

"I wasn't sure until now. But I am convinced. You know all the victims."

"Not the Zimmermans."

"You once lived in their house. Something of your presence would have still been there. The Zimmermans, casual acquaintances—they are the

pawns. They go first. Then come the more important pieces: Jacob and I, who are your guides; your
friends, your teacher, your mumma and poppa."

"Mumma and Poppa?" Starbright laughed.
"Nah!"

"Yes, Starbright. Judy and Simon Connor are
having the dreams. You must have noticed changes
in them. Tired? Irritable? Afraid?"

"They're okay," Starbright said. "I'd know if
they were sick."

"The most important chess piece is the queen. If
the queen falls, the Dream Eater will conquer the
king. Who is your queen, Starbright?"

Starbright stared at the woman, and her stomach muscles made a knot that tightened all the way
to her throat. She could not answer.

"When you know that, you will understand
what the Dream Eater is doing. Fear is the weakness, Starbright. It is only your fear that will give
the Dream Eater access to you. Think carefully. Are
you afraid for your family?"

Starbright looked away from the woman's red
staring eyes. She was remembering Esther's photo
in the dream book, remembering how she had
reacted to it with the roar of the lion. There was
no lion roar in her now, just a painfully clenched

stomach and the urge to run out of the motel room.

"I dreamed about Esther in a coffin," she said. "I wasn't afraid. I wanted to fight."

"Fight?"

"I got angry. I roared."

The woman nodded and said, "Tell me more about your dreams."

She began with the first dream and the bearded man reaching out to her from the ice. When she saw pain in the woman's face, she knew that she was describing the last communication anyone would receive from Jacob Tietz. She talked about the photo book on top of the iceberg, and as she described it, she realized that the Dream Eater had been taunting her. She had believed that she was in control of her dreams, but in fact, something else had been controlling them. The night before Mark had gone into the hospital, there had been the dream of his death played many times on TV. Then, last night, she had seen Mumma and Poppa shrinking as small as cockroaches, tiny squealing things that ran out on the road and were run over by a large truck with a torn tarp on the back.

"And did you also feel angry when you saw these images?" the woman asked.

"Sure."

"Good," said the woman. "That's how you should feel. Now do you realize that this thing is trying to manipulate you?"

Starbright nodded. She swung her chair back until it rested against the wall. "I know something's happening and I'm a part of it. But it still isn't real. It's freaksome. Like another life I'm trying to live alongside this one. A makeup life."

"That's a good way of describing it," said Lena Tietz.

Starbright wobbled on two chair legs. "Exactly what is a Dream Eater?"

"No human knows. If it has some kind of physical shape, our senses don't make anything of it. Jacob saw it as a being of pure energy with a highly formed intelligence. He said it was some kind of space parasite in existence throughout the universe. It seemed that it is mostly controlled by creatures called the Guardians of the Universe. Jacob described them as angels. They know how to make the Dream Eater harmless by compressing its nucleus into a prison rock. That was what landed at Corazón. Not a meteorite at all, Jacob said. A seamless container made of a metallic substance unknown on earth."

"And that professor released it."

"He was trying to destroy it," said Lena Tietz. "I will tell you Jacob's theory. The Guardians of the Universe realized a Dream Eater had landed on earth. They were concerned but not greatly so, because the universe is held in balance, and if the parasite were let loose, then a cure would be provided. That cure was you, Starbright."

"But that's not—"

"Please listen! There isn't much time! The Guardians looked into the future as though it were the past. They discovered that earth was as barren as its neighbors. The Dream Eater had devoured all life and had reproduced, seeding itself throughout the galaxy. When they discovered this, the Guardians also saw a shadow, the second path or overlay, that suggested another possible outcome. That is why they went to the trouble of radioing a message through a time warp. The message was to be a warning before the Dream Eater landed. Jacob believed that the overlay was a definite possibility. If it wasn't, then why would the Guardians have gone to that trouble? They made a mistake, though. They translated the signal into the language of the place where the Dream Eater would land. Because of that, the message was rejected as some kind of practical joke."

"But suppose people had taken notice of the message?" said Starbright. "Suppose they'd fired the meteorite back out on a spaceship. Then everything would be okay and the warning wouldn't have been sent. You see? That's why it's so hard to believe. There are things that just don't make a speck of sense. I know it's happening, but I keep thinking it can't be real. It's as though we've all been sucked into a movie."

"What is real?" said the woman. "I tell you, real is what we have experienced. This is new, different. There is no past experience by which we can recognize it. It is part of the mystery of the universe, and Jacob always said that there was more mystery out there than fact." She stood up slowly. "Starbright, I want to tell you that I may also be in the hospital tomorrow. I would like to give you all of Jacob's research notes and photos, but there won't be time for you to go through them. There are two things you must have." She dragged a large cardboard box across the floor, then opened it and took out a smaller box and an old *National Geographic* magazine. She put both on the table and lifted the flaps of the box. "Soon after your birth, Jacob made this for you."

"For me?"

"There was a part of the prediction that puzzled him greatly. How was the Bright Star to overcome the Dream Eater? Your lack of fear was an important part of it. But the message said you would either use or fail to use the gift that you had been given. Jacob thought a long time about that gift, and he decided it had something to do with the prison rock that had held the Dream Eater. His friend Jorge Mendoza had gone through the burned-out laboratory, salvaging all the fragments of the rock he could find. Not much, I'm afraid. Most of the laboratory disintegrated in the explosion. Jacob put some rock fragments in this titanium container. He called it a dream catcher." From the box she took a short silver tube attached to a chain. It was no bigger than her fist, although it looked heavy enough. The top of the tube unscrewed, and inside were some dark-gray crumbs of rock.

"Is that all?" asked Starbright. "What's it supposed to do?"

The woman sighed. "I don't know. Jacob hopes the prison rock will control the Dream Eater. He thinks—he thought that you might be able to get the nucleus of the Dream Eater into this canister."

"Something as small as that?" Starbright said.

"The size is meaningless," said Lena Tietz.

"Because you will be working within a dream, the fixed laws of reality will not apply. The size and shape of this catcher will change with the dream. Jacob said you should wear this around your neck, and it will accompany you into the subconscious state, where you will meet the Dream Eater. One other thing." She picked up the battered *National Geographic* magazine. "Here's a full article on the Antarctic. Read it. Look at the pictures. Absorb all the images in your head so that you can go there in your sleep. The prediction said that the Dream Eater would retreat to ice halls and reach out from there. Until now the spindle sickness has been in southern latitudes. We believe that tendrils of energy reach out from the Antarctic continent, where the nucleus lies. Why there? Perhaps the nucleus needs isolation for protection. Or cold temperature. Maybe it is vulnerable in some way. Its tendrils of power go out to feed, but the core of this evil thing stays in hiding."

Starbright flicked over the pages of the magazine and saw penguins running and sliding down dark rocks, an old sepia photo of some men with a dogsled, a wall of ice blue and white above a dark sea. She said, "How do I start to look in a place as big as the Antarctic? It's a gimassive continent."

The woman sighed. "Oh yes. Bigger than the United States. All of these were questions that bothered my brother. But he was certain that you would know the answers."

"Answers?" cried Starbright. "I don't know anything!"

"Maybe not now, but the knowledge will be with you when the times comes. That's what Jacob always believed."

Starbright had grown impatient with Jacob, Jacob, Jacob, and the way things were being thrust upon her. For a moment, cold thinking took over and pushed the lion feeling aside. Hoo-diddly! If there was a connection between those events in Argentina, her dreams and the spindle sickness, it was not her responsibility. She was twelve years old. There were grown scientists and doctors who got paid millions of dollars to sort out problems like this. What were they doing? Mark was unconscious. So were Jazzy and Mrs. Keppler. Even Dan Coulter. Why hadn't somehoodlebody found a cure for the disease long before this?

Lena Tietz must have seen her thoughts on her face. "I do not doubt my brother's wisdom. Not now. He said often, Trust your feelings, trust life, trust the universe. You know what he meant by that? If someone is living as they are meant to live, they have the whole universe on their side. You won't be alone, Starbright. You can do it if you don't let fear get in the way. And in the doing, you will have answers when you need them."

"Oh sure," Starbright said. "But will someone please tell me, what am I supposed to do?"

Lena Tietz patted her hand. "Go home. Read about the Antarctic. Put Jacob's catcher around your neck. Go to sleep."

"Just like that?"

"I wish I could tell you more."

Starbright picked up the cardboard box. It was heavy. It dragged as though it were magnetized to earth. "What about you?"

"I won't be able to go to Melbourne. I shall call to see how my brother is, then I, too, shall go to sleep. I know I won't wake up. If I appear in your dream, take no notice. Ignore any frightening image. Remember that the Dream Eater will do all it can to make you scared." She walked with Starbright to the door of the motel. "Good-bye, Starbright. I don't think I'll see you again."

Starbright stood outside in the bright sunlight, holding the box and the *National Geographic* magazine to her chest. "I still don't know what I'm supposed to do!" she cried.

Lena Tietz swayed and reached out to the door-frame to steady herself. Her breath had a sweet acrid smell. "Just do your best," she said.

CHAPTER ELEVEN

The heat of the day had drained down the sky, and a small breeze was passing through, clattering the leaves of sycamores and oaks like dried-up insects. The grasses at the edge of the road were brown, feathery with old seed heads, and there was a squirrel fidgeting along a stone wall like normal. But the road was empty, not a car or bike, not a kid on a skateboard, not even a dog out on the sidewalk, and no one rode a lawn mower or called out from a porch swing. It was as though someone had turned the town upside down and shaken out all the people.

Starbright walked in the middle of the road, swinging her legs to place her feet one in front of the other between the double yellow lines. It was a slow way to walk back from the motel, but she was in no hurry. She stopped once and put down the heavy cardboard box to scratch her ankles. The sore bits left by the bungee cord had healed and were itching something frantic inside her socks.

Tree shadows stretched all the way across the road. This was the time of day that Mark did his trumpet practice, notes that shot over the fence like fireworks or else bounced low like squishy golden balls. Hoo-diddly! If you could sew all that music together, you could make yourself wings to fly from here to the faraway ocean and back. But not yesterday. Not today. Starbright kicked at the road until the toe of her sneaker peeled back from the sole. Today Mrs. Dudnelly would be crying in her kitchen and there would be TV vans outside the houses like before. A woman would balance a camera on her shoulder while a man in a space suit would ask robot questions through a microphone inside his visor. Sure they would. They had walked straight up to her just as she was stepping out for the motel.

"Hey! You're the Connor kid. You live next door to Mark Dudnelly."

"Yes?"

"Mark is your boyfriend?"

"No."

"His mother says you spend a lot of time together."

"He is a boy. He is a friend. He is not a boyfriend."

"Thank you, Starshine. Point taken, sweetie. When did you last—"

"Starbright."

"Excuse me?"

"My name is Starbright."

"Starbright, you saw Mark Dudnelly yesterday when he was feeling ill. Did he confide in you? Did he talk about his symptoms at all?"

"No."

"He didn't say anything at all to you?"

"No. He was asleep. All day."

"What about on Friday? I believe that Mark was home from school. Mrs. Dudnelly says you visited him in the afternoon."

"Yes."

"Can you tell us how he was?"

"No."

"Jasmine Collis. She was your friend too, wasn't she?"

"Is. Is my friend."

"Okay. When did you last talk to Jasmine?"

"I don't remember."

"Star—Starbright. Just relax, sweetie, and look at the camera. Your friends and your teacher are in the hospital, and it must be just awful for you, honey. But I want you to know that we've got people all over the country praying for your friends. We want to share your pain. We want to put our hearts on the line for you, sweetie. Will you talk to us?"

"No."

"Honey—"

"No, no, no! Just scrooch away, will you?"

But they had not gone and she had run past them, back into her own yard, past the house, through the garden shed, running like a hare around Poppa's stockpiles of ceramic slabs, garden stones and terra-cotta pots, through the Radomskis' place and across Third Street. There were police cars at the intersection. She had run the other way and found more police at the corner of Third and Main, and she had stepped back into the lane by the supermarket parking lot to avoid discovery. All children were supposed to stay in their homes.

The town was empty, shops closed and dead eyed, but the expanse of street was filled with the heavy noise of helicopters, two of them hovering like big insects above the rooftops. She had squinted into the sun, almost expecting a loud voice from the skies telling her to go home and stay indoors. When nothing happened, she had turned and walked to the Bella Vista Motel.

Now it didn't matter if someone saw her. She had the cardboard box under one arm, the magazine under the other; and for the first time in her life, she was walking a double yellow line on an empty road. Now and then she would think of the woman, but mostly it was Mark who filled her head. She was remembering the panic yesterday when Mrs. Dudnelly couldn't wake him, the ambulance siren so loud it swamped their voices, then the paramedics running into the Dudnelly house. They would not let Starbright go near Mark. Even Mrs. Dudnelly could not be with him in the hospital. The building that had been the X-ray unit had been cordoned off as an isolation ward, and no one but medical staff were allowed inside. All Mrs. Dudnelly could do was stand by a window with Jazzy's parents, hoping for a glimpse as they moved him around for testing.

Four people in one day. First Jazzy, then Mark, then Dan Coulter. Last night Mr. Keppler had come back from fishing to find his wife asleep and breathing funny. He had called the doctor, who told him to call an ambulance at once.

Another helicopter was beating up the air along Third Street. Starbright saw curtains pull back in the Radomskis' house and she stopped, her arms folded over the magazine and the box, her head tilted back to look at the sky. She didn't see the National Guard patrol car come up behind her, and when it stopped with its door less than an arm's length from her, she knew she was going to get it for being out and about.

The windows were dark. One rolled down about an inch, and a voice said, "You live near here, young lady?"

"Through there." She vaguely waved the magazine.

"What's your name?"

"Starbright Connor."

"Stanton Elementary, right? You know you kids are supposed to stay inside your own four walls and wait to be tested. Your parents know you're wandering around?"

"Uh-huh." All she could see in the dark window was her own reflection. "Mumma and Poppa went up to the hospital. I'm waiting for them."

"What'd you say your name was?"

"Starbright Connor."

"You ain't feeling sick, are you?"

"No."

"Well, you get yourself off home, Starbright Connor, and wait for your folks back there. There are four cases in the hospital, all connected with the school. You could be contagious. If we see you out here again, you're in deep trouble."

The window wound up, but the patrol car did not move. It sat there, its air-conditioning whirring and spitting water on the hot tar. The driver was waiting to see where she went. Starbright knew that she was being watched by a number of people as she crossed the road. There was a face in the Radomskis' kitchen window and a venetian blind at an angle in the house opposite. She groaned. Someone would tell Mumma or Poppa for sure, and she would be in trouble lickety-split for disobedience.

They had said they'd be back about five, but it was well after seven when Poppa's truck rolled up the drive and the three of them came in. Poppa was hitching his pants up over his skinny hipbones as usual, and Esther was wearing the same old paint-spattered shirt with a garden glove sticking out of the pocket like a rooster's head, and Mumma was sounding off about the hospital bathrooms being hopeless for five hundred people waiting in the emergency room for testing. "In times of crisis everybody plans big, National

Guard, half the police in the state, national television, message from the president, experts flown in from overseas, big, big, big. But who organizes little things like paper cups and toilet tissue and somewhere to buy a cup of coffee in five hours of waiting? Don't you laugh, Simon. It's little that runs the world, things like teaspoons, tissues, safety pins, needles, shoelaces."

"How is Mark?" said Starbright, half strangled by Esther's hug.

"Mumma couldn't get to the bathroom," said Poppa. "Line was too long. She had to climb in the truck and use one of Esther's birdbaths."

"Take away little and big is paralyzed," said Mumma. "I ran my last pair of stockings on a pottery sparrow." She showed them the run below the hem of her dress.

"What about Mark?"

Poppa turned and filled the kettle at the sink. "We couldn't see him."

"Not through the window?"

"They've moved his bed to make room for others coming in," said Mumma, hopping from one foot to another. "Excuse me. I need the bathroom again."

Poppa set mugs on the table and reached for a

bag of chamomile tea. "What an afternoon," he said. "If you didn't laugh, you'd cry."

"Did Mumma get tested?" Starbright asked.

"Short answer? No. More than four hundred and fifty people turned up. They had testing kits for fifty. I ask you! Anyone who is having disturbed sleeping patterns, they said. Anyone with unusual nightmares. Come to the hospital for testing. Your mumma's been having these bad dreams. I put my name down too. But I've always been a restless sleeper, you understand. We thought there might be a dozen people there. It was packed! The air-conditioning couldn't cope. The staff couldn't cope." He opened the box of cookies. "No children, you understand. They have to be tested in their own homes. But they did start with the youngest, people in their late teens, twenties."

Esther put her face close to Starbright's and put out her tongue. "Ah, ah, ah!" she said.

"Did you—" Starbright was surprised.

Poppa answered for Esther. "We got Esther done, too. When they called her age group, we thought we might as well. She's clear. Then they ran out of testing kits. More were expected, but they never arrived. Problems with the quarantine. We have to go back tomorrow."

"Ah, ah, ah!" Esther was tapping her tongue with her finger.

"They looked at your tongue?" said Starbright.

"A sample of saliva," said Poppa. "They have a wooden Popsicle stick with a chemical in it that tests your saliva. One of the symptoms, you understand, is a change in body fluids. Certain kinds of ketones, they said. It's a quick test."

Burned sugar, thought Starbright. She looked quickly at Esther, then at Poppa. "Esther's okay?"

"Everyone tested was okay." It was Mumma coming back from the bathroom and smoothing the wrinkles in her dress. "Not one positive reaction. Just goes to show how people imagine things. I tell you this: If you took a healthy person, put her in a hospital bed and started talking disease, doing tests, what do you bet that in two weeks she'd really be ill? Sickness is in the mind."

"You want some chamomile tea?" Poppa asked her.

"Why not?" she said. "It won't make any difference." She sat in a chair and rubbed her hands over her face. "One hundred percent negative, and there's all those people thinking they might have spindle sickness. You see what crazy talk can do?"

"Cookie, Mumma?" said Esther, holding out the

box. "Good cookie, Mumma?"

A coldness struck Starbright, the steely alertness that came to her at times of danger, but it was a few seconds before she realized what had caused it. Mumma's eyes! They were pink and red around the rims. Starbright went quiet from head to foot. But maybe it was because Mumma was tired. Hoodiddly, if you were scared of spindle sickness, you would get bad dreams, right? And if you got bad dreams, you would try to stay awake and get tired. Right? And if you got tired, your eyes got red.

As Mumma reached into the box for a cookie, Starbright gave her a hug. She leaned all the way around to kiss Mumma on the cheek, and as she did so, she breathed in deep and caught it through Mumma's rose perfume. There was no mistaking that burned-sugar smell.

"Love you, sweetheart," said Mumma, giving her a squeeze.

Starbright looked up at Poppa. His eyes, too, were tired, watering a little, red rimmed. "Hug for Poppa too," she said, and she went to him.

He ruffled her hair and laughed, and his breath, too, had the same sweet chemical odor.

"Hug Esther too. Hug Esther, hug Esther. Please, Starbright, baby." Esther's eyes were glowing with health and laughter. Starbright ran into her arms, and the cold feeling left her as she inhaled the warm grassy fragrance of Esther's breath, a smell she had always known. Esther was clear, all right. She rested her head on Esther's shoulder and let the fuzzy warmth of her hug flow through her. It was the kind of warmth that clicked your bones back into place, smoothed out your muscles and made your blood sing a soft lullaby all the way around your body.

"Looks like Sue Dudnelly is home," said Poppa. He was on his toes and leaning over the kitchen bench toward the window. "There's another car with her. More reporters, I guess. They've been thick as flies all day."

Mumma bit her cookie and said, in a shower of crumbs, "Mark will be okay. It's not spindle sickness. With the Zimmermans it was age. The kids have got something else. They don't know anything, so why are they trying to scare people?"

"We'd better go over and see how she is," said Poppa. "We'll wait until the reporters have gone."

"I won't go," said Starbright.

They looked at her. "You sure, honey?" said Mumma. "She might have some news."

"I'm going to bed," Starbright said.

CHAPTER TWELVE

The warmth of Esther's hug did not last long. Starbright was cold again, her body like a strong machine, springs coiled and tense, her mind set on a path that had no feeling attached to it, only an alertness that acted like a radar for danger. She had always been like this. Perhaps it was what the woman had meant by having no fear. She did not know. In this state, she always saw clearly between right and wrong, although the rightness and wrongness might not be as others judged them. When she was confronted with a wrongdoing, a feeling came to her that was also cold, an icy anger that made her strength expand and burst out into action.

She stood in front of the mirror in her pajamas, staring at her reflection. Maybe this was how lions felt when they were hunting through tall grasses on the African plains: muscles tight as steel, brain flashing signals, yes, no, left, right, stop, start. She leaned toward the mirror, almost expecting her dark eyes to turn yellow around pinpoints of pupils. They didn't, but she knew they felt like lion's eyes. The hunt was about to begin.

Suddenly, she laughed out loud and began scratching at the flaking skin on her ankles. What a lot of bunhiddly hoozit! She was Starbright Connor and this was all playacting. She was only doing it because of Mark and Jazzy and poor old Mrs. Okay. And Mumma and Poppa. Just in case. Anything was worth a try.

She got into bed and, again, studied the *National Geographic* magazine. The Antarctic story covered the trail of Captain Robert Falcon Scott and his attempt to reach the South Pole. With the old sepia-colored pictures of sober-faced men, there were colored photos of penguins gallumping into the water, flocks of nesting birds and glaciers of blue-and-white ice scarred with deep crevasses. She stared at the pages until the pictures were branded on her brain; then she reached down beside her bed for the silver metal tube and chain. Ridicunonsity! she thought. Pure skrinkleshank unreal. The tube rattled as though it were full of bones when she put the chain over her head. Some necklace! The dream catcher was far too heavy to lie on her chest, and she had to shift it sideways so that it fitted on the mattress under her arm. With the other arm, she could just reach the bedside light.

"Snow and ice," she said to the darkness. "Dogsled. Ship stuck in pack ice. Crevasse. Glacier. Icicles. Blizzard." But it was difficult to keep an active mind on one line of thought. As she lay there describing out loud the Antarctic photographs, her mind was wandering to other scenes: Mark's white face, Mrs. Dudnelly's tears, the woman in the motel, the double road lines beneath her feet and the National Guard car pulling up alongside with its air-conditioning whirring. The car was newly polished, and the sun, low in the sky, spun like fire on its hood. She could see her face in the dark window, and yes, now her eyes were definitely yellow. The rest of her face and hair were the same, but it was a lion's gaze that looked back at her, and she said to herself, Uh-oh, I've done it. I've gone to sleep with the wrong thought picture.

There wasn't much she could do about it except turn her back to the car and walk on, pretending it wasn't there. The metal tube swung across her chest with every step. It had not changed in size and shape as the woman had suggested, but it was definitely lighter and she did not have to support it with her hands. The car cruised quietly behind her. She glanced over her shoulder and saw that, although all its windows were closed, the glass was no longer dark. There was a clear view of the interior of the car, front seats and back, and there was no one in it.

She stopped. The car stopped. She put her hands on her hips and looked at it. "You should know by now that I find your games very boring," she said.

Nothing came from the car, not even a flicker of lightning, but slowly, it began to roll backward.

"You know why I am here," she said as the car retreated. "You know what I am going to do." She hesitated, because in truth she didn't have any idea of what she was going to do, or even say. The woman's words came to her, a faint memory from outside her dream, and she shouted, "I am going to find your heart and destroy it. The universe is on my side!"

The car was now at a distance, but it was not going away. It stopped. There was the sound of a gear shift, a turn of the wheels toward her, then the engine roared. She laughed, raised her arms and lifted herself into the air as the car rushed past beneath her feet. The wind of its attack fluttered her pajamas and hair.

"Nice try!" she shouted after it.

She was on the road again, but now the way was empty and it went on forever. The trees on either side had disappeared, replaced by swampland that extended as far as the horizon. The sky had grown dark with clouds, and the familiar lightning was flickering like snakes' tongues overhead. She marched on, deliberately swinging her arms, feeling the *clink, clink* of the rocks inside the tube as it swung on her chest. She started to whistle "Yankee Doodle," but that old Dream Eater wind came up and blew the notes away from her mouth, so she just smiled instead to let it know she didn't care.

Then, somewhere distant, she heard someone else whistling "Yankee Doodle." She stopped to listen and realized that it was a trumpet sound, coming from the swamp to her right. She could actually see the notes rising as golden bubbles from the reeds and swamp grass.

"Mark?" she called. "Mark—you there?"

The notes bubbled up joyfully in reply, wonderful trills that shone against the dark sky. They were coming closer, skating toward her across the pondweed and the dark oily waters.

"Mark? Where are you?" She was at the edge of

the road, bending over, looking down at the water and the music bubbles that came up and burst around her ears. "Mark?"

She saw the trumpet first. It rose from the surface, shining gold and dripping. Then out came a skeleton. The eye sockets were filled with Mark's reddened eyes, and there was a small patch of ginger hair on the skull. The trumpet was clamped against the bony grin.

Starbright's smile disappeared and cold anger filled her face. "You have many disguises," she said to the skeleton. "But believe me, I will find the heart of who you are."

The skeleton trilled a few trumpet notes and its other hand shot out. At the same time, Starbright realized that she was leaning over with the metal tube dangling within the skeleton's grasp. She pulled back as the fingers closed on the chain. "No!" she cried in her lion roar.

Her voice sent a great shiver through the creature. The trumpet fell into the swamp and disappeared. The bones went on shaking until they came apart and fell into the water, where they floated like small sticks. She was left with three fingers hooked around the chain on the tube. She broke the joints apart and pulled them off, threw them after the rest of the bones. They made a small splash and bobbed in a circle of ripples.

"You'll have to do better than that!" she bellowed at the lightning that crackled across the sky.

The swamp turned into the sea, deep blue and ruffled, floating with small bits of seaweed, extending to the horizon on either side, but the road remained the same, a straight gray line that went as far as the eye could see. Starbright walked along the central yellow line, one foot in front of the other. She was sure that she was supposed to be in some other place but could not remember where. Pictures, she said to herself. Photos. Photos of what?

The clouds moved fast overhead, purple and gray, and the lightning played across them in scribbled patterns. She guessed that while the Dream Eater could turn itself into anything, its true self was most like lightning. Pure energy, the woman had said.

The moment she thought about the woman, Lena Tietz appeared at her side. She was wearing the same clothes she'd had on at the motel, but now she didn't look so sick. Her gray hair was not stuck to her head. It bounced out, full and frizzy as she walked. Her browny-green eyes were clear behind the glasses, and she was smiling. "Do you mind if I walk with you?" she said.

Starbright felt a cold alertness as she remembered the words in the motel. *If I appear in your dream, take no notice.* She did not reply but looked straight ahead and increased her speed.

"I'm stuck in my dream, Starbright. I can't wake up. I told you that, didn't I? No doubt tomorrow someone will find me at the motel and take me to the hospital, but it won't do any good. I'm finished."

Starbright wanted to glance back at her but didn't. She heard the soft *pat-pat* of the woman's sandals on the road behind her.

"I thought," said Lena Tietz, "that if I am going to be stuck in a dream, I might as well make it your dream. I could come across to help you. After all, I am supposed to be your guide."

Starbright was twitching with alertness, but she knew that it was possible to share someone else's dream. She and Mark had done it. "How do I know you are you?" she asked.

There was a soft sigh that had a smile in it. "I could describe to you my motel room with the orange-and-brown wallpaper. I could tell you about Jacob dying in a Melbourne hospital. I could go over, word by word, our conversation today and my warning that if I appeared in your dream, you were to take no notice."

At that, Starbright turned to look at her. The woman's smile was warm and apologetic. "I know I said that to you. It was before I realized I might be of some use."

"What kind of use?" Starbright asked.

"I honestly don't know. But two heads are better than one, and maybe the knowledge will come when it's needed. I'm positive the universe will look after us."

That convinced Starbright. She stopped and returned the woman's smile with a welcoming grin. "Sure," she said. "Thanks heaps. I could use some help."

Lena Tietz smiled almost shyly. "You will need to tell me what to do. I rely on your judgment."

Starbright took the chain off her aching neck and lifted it over her head. "Will you carry this for a while? It's gotten very heavy."

"I thought it would change," said the woman. "Nothing is fixed in dreams."

"It was light to begin with," said Starbright. "Now it's really hurting my neck and ribs."

Lena Tietz did not put the chain around her own neck but carried it in her hand, swinging the tube a few inches off the ground. "Let me know when you want it back," she said.

As they walked on together, it seemed to Starbright that the journey was easier. She felt lighter, the sky was brighter, the sea as calm as blue milk. She said to Lena Tietz, "There is something else you can help me with. I'm not meant to be on this road. You told me about another place, but I don't remember."

"Oh?"

"It's got something to do with photos. A book."

"I'm sure you will remember," said Lena Tietz. "All in good time. Starbright, I'm carrying your dream catcher, but I also carry a psychological burden. I must share it with you. It concerns my brother."

"You told me the place was important," insisted Starbright. "Photos. Pictures. It's where I'm supposed to go."

"Are you listening to me, Starbright? My brother, Jacob, was a romantic. He had an active imagination. Starbright, I have to tell you. There is no such thing as an overlay. Jacob made that up."

"What?"

"The warning is true, but there is no hope. Not for you, for me, for the world. I am sorry that I misled you. Your journey will fail."

Starbright turned, and the cold anger grew inside her. "What are you talking about?" She looked at the frizzy gray hair, the smudged glasses, the eyes glassy with tears. "You know where I am supposed to be," she insisted. "If you were Lena Tietz, you would tell me."

The woman shook with sobs, and the tears ran down her wrinkled cheeks. "I am so sorry, Starbright."

"Give me that dream catcher!" Starbright roared. But as she leaped forward, the woman stepped back and swung her arm. The silver chain whirled in a blurred circle. The tube arced high into the sky, up, up beyond any human throw. It streaked through the air with the chain behind it, then came down. Starbright saw the distant splash in the sea.

"So sorry, Starbright." The woman's sobs were now laughter. "So sorry, baby, sorry, sorry, bright star baby."

"No!" Starbright leaped at the thing that looked like Lena Tietz but sounded like Esther. Her hands closed on air as the woman dissolved into a gray cloud and floated away on laughter.

Now there was laughter everywhere, in the sea,

on the road, laughter in the wind that swept the cloud to shreds, laughter crackling like electricity.

"There is no such thing as an overlay," howled the laughter.

The lion roar came up in Starbright. She stood in the road with her fists clenched, her head back. "Liar!" she yelled.

CHAPTER THIRTEEN

Starbright understood that dreams did not operate according to waking rules. Objects were not fixed, and neither was time. When she could not imagine the dream catcher back out of the sea, she decided to get it another way. She would turn and walk back the way she had come until she got to the point in the road where she had met the figure of the nurse. That would take her to the place in her dream where she still had the catcher around her neck.

Almost as soon as she started retracing her steps, she saw the truck. She felt a rush of warmth as she recognized the three figures sitting inside it. Mumma driving, Esther in the middle, Poppa, thin as a drinking straw, waving out his window. She heard their voices shrill with excitement as they came near.

"Starbright! Hey, Starbright! Want a ride?"

Immediately, the cold feeling took over. She

stopped and yelled, "No! Go away!"

The truck stopped. She could see their faces, concerned and puzzled. Mumma banged her hand on the outside of her door, hitting it like a drum. "We've come all this way to give you a lift. We can't go back."

Then Starbright saw that the road behind the truck was dipping down into the sea. It was true. They could not go back and neither could she. That way, the entire road was now underwater.

She knew that she was being deceived by an illusion. "You are not my family!" she yelled. "You're the Dream Eater! Get off my road!"

The truck was slipping backward, down the hill toward the sea. There was a piercing scream from Esther, and Mumma cried, "Starbright! Do something! It's the brakes!"

"Starbright!" called Poppa. "Help us!"

Starbright put her hands over her ears, but she could not block out the sight of their faces as the truck slid into the sea. The last thing she saw was Esther's terrified eyes and open mouth, and then the truck disappeared under the surface, leaving ripples and bubbles. She stared at the point where the water lapped across the road and felt the hugeness of her icy anger. How dare this thing use images of her family to trap her!

When she turned away to resume her journey, it seemed that the anger had made her grow, so instead of being a twelve-year-old girl on a road, she was now a giant planting huge bare feet on a narrow path. The sky stretched like a gray rubber sheet over her head, and lightning flickered around her ears, but she strode through it. The coldness of her anger formed words that fell with every footstep, ice, snow, sleet, blizzard, and gradually the words began to form pictures in her head. Ice, snow, blizzard, crevasse. And there it was. The place. Laid out in her head, layers of white, ready for her to step into it. The Antarctic continent. Oh yes, that was it. And not just anywhere in the Antarctic but the one special place where the heart of the Dream Eater lay.

The pictures in her mind were powerful, and she knew that in a moment she would be in them. But then her ankles began to itch. Even in her dream those wangling bungee-cord scars were a distraction. She bent over, a long way down for a giant, and then saw what was causing the itch. Not the scars. Crawling over her bare feet and ankles were hundreds of cockroaches. They were huge. Their brown bodies shone, their feet scuttled and scratched over her toes, their antennae twitched.

"Yeech!" she screamed. She lifted a foot and shook it. Brown bodies fell in all directions. When she put the foot down again, cockroaches crunched under her bare sole and stuck between her toes. One bug, half squashed, was trying to struggle up over her big toenail.

She could not stop screaming. She shook the other foot. The twitching bugs flew like a shower of hard rain, some hitting her face and hair. She put her foot down and again felt the crunch as cock-roaches, as crisp as popcorn, broke and squished out their insides against her skin. She covered her face with her hands.

"Get off me! Get off me!" she shrieked.

Her heart was beating so fast, she thought that her chest would explode. She was no longer a giant. She was sliding down to a smallness as her strength left her, down close to the seething mass of insects. She took her hands away from her face and discovered that a fresh horde of cockroaches was swarming over her feet. They were everywhere. "No, no!" she bellowed, sobbing and shaking. "Oh, please no!"

Then, suddenly, behind her scream, there came a small memory. It was a still point in her terror, something shining in her head like a warm light. She gasped, swallowed a sob and focused on it. It was a memory of Esther sitting at the table with a dead cockroach in her hand. She could see Esther stroking its back very gently with her little finger as though it were a treasure. "Lovesee," Esther was saying. "Beautiful lovesee."

Starbright closed her eyes and mouth and held her breath. She was seeing the pages of cockroach paintings, each bug as beautiful as a jewel, and hearing Esther's voice so close that it filled up her head. Beautiful lovesee. Beautiful lovesee. But beyond those words, the cockroaches were trying to crawl up her legs. She let her breath out without a sound, opened her eyes and tried to pretend that she was Esther.

The creatures that ran over her were like small brown cars heaped up in a traffic jam. Their bodies shone as though they had been enameled. She took another breath, a deep intake of air that filled her lungs; then she bent at the knees and put her hand down. She would pick one up if it killed her.

Cockroaches ran over her fingers and over her palm. Some fell off as she brought her hand closer to her face. Their backs were shining, little suits of armor polished with light. They had legs like fine black wire, and their feelers were delicately feathered, curved, moving as gracefully as the arms of a ballet dancer. Yes, she supposed that someone could actually say they were beautiful. She turned her hand over to let a cockroach run over the backs of her knuckles, and after a while, she began to understand why Esther had admired these insect machines, why she had wanted to paint them. They were finely made, and no doubt if they were some rare threatened species from the Amazon jungle, everyone would admire them.

Beautiful lovesee, Esther had said. Now Starbright knew what that meant. See with the eyes of love and a thing becomes beautiful. See with the eyes of hate and things are ugly.

It was not the cockroaches that had been ugly, but her vision of them.

Gently, Starbright let the cockroach back to the ground and crouched there, still as a rock, lest she tread on more of them. She even began to enjoy the tickling sensation of their legs on her feet.

"You know what?" she said to the insects. "I've got this sister who is my mother, and she's the first person I ever heard say a cockroach was beautiful. You are. You're really pretty, and I'm sorry I trod on some of you." Slowly, carefully, she stood up.

The feeling of panic had gone, and so had the cold anger. For some reason, it seemed important to her to tell the cockroaches about Esther. "Some people think she's dumb because she can't read or write or talk much. But hoo-diddly, she knows all the important stuff that the rest of the world hasn't learned in thousands of years. It's not just you guys. She thinks everything's beautiful. Even the fuzzy mold on bread. She jumps up and down and claps her hands and calls it garden bread. She really is something. You know that, cockroaches?"

But they were no longer cockroaches around her feet. They were dried leaves blowing away in a cold wind, and now in front of her was the white land she had seen in her thoughts, as clean as the first page of an unwritten book. The road beneath her disappeared. She was floating off the snowy ground, arms spread like a bird over as many shapes of white as could be imagined. The blue sky outlined mountain cones with wrinkled glaciers, and as she flew, white plains rippled in front of her, snow folding and unfolding like some never-ending bridal garment. Steep bluffs sparkled over the rough pack ice of the sea. Farther out, icebergs floated as tall as marble castles. Over everything she could see, and now beneath her, lines of blue and green lightning shone like Christmas decorations.

The breeze that flapped her pajamas and hair was so cold that it burned her cheeks, but she was no longer cold inside. Something had happened. The roaring lion had gone. What she did feel within her was the singing sensation that came with one of Esther's hugs.

She remembered that she had said to Lena Tietz that she didn't know where to look in Antarctica for the Dream Eater. It's a gimassive continent, she had cried, and Lena Tietz had said that the knowing would come with the doing. The doing also came with the knowing, and the way was actually very easy. All that was needed was to fly along the lightning lines that flickered and rippled back to their source like converging roads on a map. From a distance she could see where the lines came together. They thickened until they completely covered the snow, then they fell, like a circular waterfall, into the deep dish of a crevasse.

As she drifted closer, she saw, in the center of the crevasse, a red glow that flickered as though there were a fire at the heart of the lightning. Closer still, she saw that light came from a red shape that pulsed like a naked brain in the bottom of the steep-sided pit. The knowledge was certain.

This was the nucleus of the Dream Eater. From it extended the thousands of filaments that crackled across the snow to disappear on the horizon in every direction.

Starbright hovered high above the crevasse. The snow inside glowed deep red, and icicles hung like tongues of fire near the Dream Eater's nucleus, which seemed to change shape as she looked. One moment it was like a brain, the next a red eye, then a throbbing jelly as transparent as red water. The lightning that left the heart changed from red to orange to yellow to green and blue as it whipped away across the icefield.

Now some of the tendrils came up from the snow to wrap themselves around Starbright. They did not touch her. But her head was full of the noise of their crackling.

She looked directly down at the nucleus of the space parasite that lay like some extraordinary jelly-fish with filaments spread out across the snow, and she was surprised at her feeling. "You are beautiful too!" she said. "You are! Really beautiful!"

The lightning spun hissing threads about her but did not touch her. When she moved, the lightning also moved. She did not doubt what she had to do. She said to the Dream Eater in a voice that filled the crevasse, "I am sorry I hated you. Everything has to eat to live, and you were only doing what we all do, feeding yourself. If you're evil, then I reckon chickens and cows and fish think I'm evil too." She floated down. "But this isn't your planet, Dream Eater. You'll have to go."

Now she was at the bottom of the crevasse and level with the red globe. All around her was such a storm of lightning that she could barely see for the seething net of electric threads.

"Release their energy, Dream Eater," she said loudly. "The people you are feeding on. Let them go!" And she reached her hands through the lightning to the heart of the Dream Eater.

She never did touch it. There was a great roaring sound hammering her ears. The ice heaved and splintered, and she was thrown upward in a shower of blue and white, her arms and legs outstretched. Her back arched. For a second she seemed to hang in a cloud of glittering particles, then she landed with a thump on her back at the edge of the crevasse. A rain of ice fell around her. At the same time, the red globe shot into the air, trailing threads of lightning. It whooshed away like a rocket, so fast that within five seconds it was a thin streak of red in a sky filled with stars. The crevasse in front of

Starbright was now a deep dark pit.

She lay on her back in the crunch of powdered snow and ice and gazed at the sky. When had daylight turned to night? A moment ago the sun had been shining. But that was the way with dreams. The sky was clear. No gray and purple cloud. No wind. No lightning. "I'm sorry," she whispered as the red dot disappeared in space. "But it had to be." She was quiet for a while, feeling the snow under her, the endless sky above; then the song surged through her blood again, and she called to the vast emptiness. "The twins were wrong! Both wrong! The metal tube was not the gift I needed. The gift was Esther. The gift was lovesee!"

And she woke up shouting, "Lovesee!" to a bedroom filled with sunshine.

She sat up in bed and looked at the time. It was 9:20 A.M., and the house echoed with daytime noises: the washing machine *thump-thump-thumping* in the laundry room and Poppa talking on the phone. She felt about her neck and then her bed for the metal tube on the chain. It was gone, clean hoozit vanished. But the *National Geographic* magazine was still under her pillow.

"You call, sweetheart?" Mumma was at the door,

sleeves rolled up above her elbows, gardening apron on. Her eyes were bright and clear, no redness, no dark smudges.

"I just saw the time," Starbright said.

"Don't worry a speck about that," said Mumma. "We all slept late this morning. But there's good news about the herbicide business. The kids are getting out of the hospital this morning. Mrs. Dudnelly just called."

Starbright leaped out of bed. "Mark is okay?"

"Oh sure. He had a bit of a headache last night, but his mom says that's not the weed killer. He's been eating big-time the candy his friends brought him."

"Last night?" Starbright stared at her. "Mumma, last night Mark was unconscious. Spindle sickness."

"Spindle what?" Mumma came into the room and picked up some clothes. "Oh, look at this! Starbright, if you're going to hang your good clothes on the floor, you can iron them yourself."

"Mark and Jazzy." Starbright rubbed her head, trying to separate yesterday from her dream. "Mrs. Keppler. Dan Coulter. It was on TV—"

"Oh, they'll be out today too." Mumma put the dress on a hanger. "But they've delayed the opening of school another two days. They're having to lift every bit of grass that was sprayed. Just imagine it. With all the warnings about these things, you'd think they'd have more sense than to go spraying a new weed killer on the school grounds. Seems the more they test the stuff, the more they find out how toxic it is." Mumma put her hands on her hips. "You want to eat now so I can clean up the breakfast things?"

Starbright went into the kitchen in her pajamas and sat at the table. She was feeling confused, her head still in a place that was more real than Mumma's talk of weed spray. What was happening? Mark had been in a coma, hadn't he? Sure he had.

She poured orange juice into a glass and fished out a seed with her finger. Poppa was pacing in and out with his cell phone against his ear, looking up books with the other hand, writing on order forms, jotting down dates. The TV on the refrigerator was equally loud, so it and Poppa seemed to be in some kind of argument. Starbright focused on the miniature screen and the newscaster with her fresh red lipstick. She, too, was going on about weed killer.

"—three students and their teacher, who were admitted to Stanton Hospital with severe headaches and vomiting, were suffering from the toxic effects of TD9-40, the herbicide marketed under the name Blitzweed. Doctors at Stanton say the patients are well on the way to recovery and show no enduring ill effects. TD9-40 was withdrawn from the market almost a week ago, when it was suspected of causing respiratory failure in an elderly Claircomb couple. But late on Thursday, Stanton School District workers, who failed to connect TD9-40 with the brand name Blitzweed, went on to spray weeds at Stanton school while four persons were still on the grounds—"

Poppa squeaked the OFF button on his phone, folded it and put it in his jeans pocket. "Hi, sleepyhead! Mumma tell you that Mark is coming home this morning?"

Starbright crouched over her cornflakes. "Weed spray," she said. "Right?"

Poppa laughed. "Gives our business a boost. They used to look sideways at us, you understand. They thought we were crazy with our organic methods and our steam and gas flame weed burners. Now we've got so many calls coming in, we're going to have to hire help. There you are!" He pointed to his pocket and the phone that was beeping in it, then he walked away, unfolding the phone and saying, "Good morning. This is Simon Connor."

Starbright finished her cornflakes, put her bowl

in the dishwasher and went outside. The morning was already warm, and the smell of roses and lavender filled the air. Esther was on her knees by the potting shed, mixing peat, compost and sand for the seedling trays. Pushkin was walking back and forth through the rich black mixture, arching his back and tail and rubbing his head against Esther's jeans. She worked her trowel around him, pausing every now and then to stroke his head or cheek. When she saw Starbright, she dropped the trowel and stood up, wiping dirt off her hands and onto her T-shirt. Starbright ran to her and threw her arms around her. Esther laughed and jiggled.

Starbright held Esther's arms and moved back a step. "Lovesee," she said.

Esther stopped laughing. She put her head on one side, like a bird, and looked at Starbright with dark shining eyes. "Baby lovesee," she said.

Starbright shook her gently. "Esther, things have changed. I think it's something to do with the overlay. But you know about the spindle sickness, don't you, Esther. You've known all along about the Dream Eater?"

Esther's expression did not alter, but she began to rock back and forth as she sometimes did, humming a small tuneless song. After a while she stopped and said, "Poppa no remember, Mumma no remember, Mark no remember, baby lady no remember, Poppa no remember, Mumma—"

Starbright let go of her arms. "But you remember! You do, don't you, Esther? You and I both remember! You are my gift!"

Esther's smile remained the same, her eyes a dark secret of knowing or unknowing. Starbright could not tell, but she tried again. "Lovesee!" she said.

Esther brushed her hair away from her face and got down on her knees again. She picked up her trowel. "Different now. Poppa no remember, Mumma no remember. Just Esther. Just baby lovesee."

"You knew all the time, didn't you?" said Starbright. "You've always known." She squatted down so that her face was close to Esther's. "Who are you, Esther? I know you're my mother, but what else are you?"

Esther did not look at her. "Busy seedgrow. Busy, busy, busy," she said. She scratched the cat under his chin. "Busy seedgrow, puss, puss." Then she went on mixing the rich soil with an easy rocking motion, humming as she worked.

CHAPTER FOURTEEN

Mark had never heard of spindle sickness. He thought it was another of Starbright's made-up words.

She sat on the spare bed in his room, picking at a scab on her ankle, wondering how much of last week he had forgotten. Esther's butterfly painting was on his bulletin board hanging from a thumbtack in the top right corner. She said, "I told you Esther was my mother?"

"Yeah, yeah." He shrugged. "You're not still mad about that?"

"No."

"Okay then." He settled back against his pillows and grinned. "They shot me full of this dye that went right through me and then they X-rayed my kidneys. They needed to know if there was any damage." He laughed. "You wouldn't believe all the tests they did! They kept coming with this needle like a big mosquito." He reached for some grapes from the bowl beside his bed. "Did you see my name in the paper?"

"Sure. And Jazzy's and Dan's and Mrs. Keppler's."

"Mom's kept all the cuttings. She says the Blitzweed company is going to pay all the hospital bills and buy new grass for the school. Want a grape?"

She shook her head. It was hot in the room. The sun poured in the window, and a fly buzzed up and down the glass. She said, "Last Monday, did Mrs. Keppler talk about spindle—about the weedkiller sickness?"

"Hmm?" His mouth was full of grapes.

"Did she tell us about it in class?"

He swallowed. "Last Monday? How could she? It wasn't sprayed on the school till Thursday. It's a miracle only three of us were sick."

"Four," she said, scratching her ankle.

"Oh yeah, Mrs. Okay. I was forgetting her. What's the matter? You got fleas or something?"

"It's where that flippy bungee cord chafed my skin. It itches."

"Your mumma and poppa know yet you did that?"

"Sort of. Well, no, not every detail."

Mark turned away. He had seen the fly crawling over the window. He rolled up a computer magazine, knelt on the bed and leaned toward the glass. *Thwack!* He missed. He raised the magazine again.

"No! Stop!" cried Starbright.

He looked at her, the magazine held over his shoulder.

"You don't have to kill it!" she said. She reached past him and opened the window. The fly went out, zigzagging into the garden. "You want this left open?" she asked.

"Close it. I might get a chill." He threw the magazine onto his bed, where it uncurled. "Since when have you been running Operation Fly Rescue? Those things are swarming with bacteria. That'll go out and breed and come back in the thousands." He pulled the covers up to his chin. "You going to tell them about the bungee jump?"

"Probably." She scratched her ankle again. "You're right, Mark. It was dangerous. I shouldn't have done it."

He smiled and folded his hands behind his head. Then he said, "Did I tell you they did a brain scan? Because of the headache. You never know if there's some kind of hemorrhage in cases like this, but when they told me, shoot, I thought they were going to shave all my hair off."

"Did you have any bad dreams?" she asked.

"Dreams?" He thought for a moment. "Can't remember. They gave me stuff to make me sleep." Then he shook his head. "Nope. No bad dreams."

Starbright discovered that not only was spindle sickness gone from people's memory, there was no record of it anywhere in the newspapers. She spent an hour in the public library, going through the papers of the past week, and found nothing. There was a lot about the herbicide TD9-40. The spray was already under investigation when weeds around the bus stop at Claircomb had been sprayed. The elderly couple living next door had become seriously ill. Because spraying had been done the same weekend at the district schools and community college in Claircomb, those had been closed. There was a total ban announced on the use of TD9-40. Another newspaper report had the headline "WEED SPRAY LOVEBIRDS DIE TOGETHER AFTER 65 YEARS OF MARRIAGE." Then, in Saturday's paper, there was the big news, the spraying of Stanton school grounds late Thursday afternoon by a group of workers who did not know, they said, that Blitzweed was TD9-40. Three students and a teacher in the school at the time had inhaled the spray. They had become ill and were hospitalized Saturday morning. The rest of the staff and students who were at the school the day after the spraying were, so far, showing no ill effects.

Nowhere was there anything about spindle sickness.

Starbright talked to Mrs. Brianna LaVal, the librarian, who was a lot like a library herself, pages and pages of knowledge stuffed inside a big-chested dress of yellow sunflowers. "Argentina," she said to Mrs. LaVal. "Australia."

"Sorry, Starbright. I've never heard of it."

"What about South Africa?"

"Not South Africa," said Mrs. LaVal. "I've got some family over there, cousin has a shoe factory in the Cape, more cousins farming up north. They keep in touch. I positively would know if there was any epidemic. Now, you are sure you got the right name? Maybe there is some other medical term? Why don't you search one of the computers?"

There was no spindle sickness on the computers either. Starbright did, however, find a list of astro-nomical observatories, and hoo-diddly, there it was, El Único Observatory near Buenos Aires. Quickly she punched the keys to bring it up on the screen. Yes, yes, a photo of the observatory similar to the photocopied picture in Jacob Tietz's article. She leaned forward to read about it, then slumped back in the library chair. The only real information was that, in 1978, the observatory was the first in the southern hemisphere to install a Galileo SP 300 telescope. Beneath that was the name of the director of El Único Observatory, Professor Eduardo Camino de Cruz, 1932–   . Starbright knew what that dash meant followed by nothing. Professor Camino de Cruz was still alive.

There had been no explosion, no meteorite, no warning. The time shift had happened, and the Dream Eater had not existed.

She looked up the UFO Society and, as she suspected, there were no references to the meteorite. She closed the computer down and for a while sat staring at the blank screen. She, too, was different, as though some change had taken place inside her as well. There was a quietness inside her, a sense of something finished. It was as though she had been studying for twelve years for an exam, and now it was over.

The memories of the last eight days, in and out of

dreams, were clear in her head, every detail sharp as cut glass. Now the events seemed not like a movie, but like the most real thing that had ever happened to her. Yet they were real only to her and Esther. Yeah, sure they were real to Esther. But she would probably never find out how much Esther knew.

Suddenly, she pushed back the chair. Graggles and beans! She still had the *National Geographic* magazine with the Antarctic pictures. That hadn't changed. She had looked at it again this morning. And if that was the same, it must mean that the rest of Jacob Tietz's stuff was unchanged, the files, the notes, the yellow envelope.

"You look as though you found something," said Mrs. LaVal as she walked by.

"I think so," Starbright said, jumping out of the chair. "I really think so."

The nurse's small car was still outside the motel, but the passenger door was open and the large box of papers was on the seat. Before Starbright got to the motel doorway, Lena Tietz came out, carrying a suitcase. She did not look sick. She was wearing her bright-pink blouse and a blue skirt. Her step was firm, her smile bright. "Oh, it's—it's— No, let me think. The girl who is interested in my brother's research."

"Starbright."

"Yes, Starbright." The woman put down her suitcase. "I'm sorry. I've had a lot on my mind lately. My memory is awful."

Starbright held out the *National Geographic*. "I brought back the magazine, but I'm afraid I don't have the dream catcher."

The woman did not take the magazine but instead frowned and put her hand to her forehead. "But I'm sure you gave me the dream catcher," she said.

Starbright took a quick breath. "You remember!" she cried.

"Oh, yes, I am sure of it. It's here somewhere." Lena Tietz went to the car and began searching in the box on the seat. "Forgive me, I've been a little unwell. Yes, yes! I knew it! You gave it back to me with my brother's magazine article." She turned around, and in her hand was an object that Starbright had not seen before. It was a hoop about eight inches in diameter, wrapped in soft leather. In the center of the hoop there was a web of thread with beads attached. More beads and feathers hung from the outside of the hoop. "See? You returned it. Jacob's Navajo dream catcher."

Starbright stood still, the *National Geographic* in her hand.

Lena Tietz put the dream catcher back in the box. "Did I tell you that Jacob had malaria? He got it in Malaysia and they sent him back to Australia. He's getting better, but we're twins, you see. When one of us gets sick, the other tends to echo the symptoms." She smiled at Starbright and spread her arms to indicate the motel. "It's not the best place to spend a week of your vacation, is it? But I did feel poorly. I couldn't go on driving. Never mind, I got a good rest and there was a bonus. I met you. It's not often one comes across a child interested in Native American spirituality." She took the magazine. "Did you read it?"

"Antarctica," Starbright said slowly.

"What? Oh no, no, no! The native peoples of the Lake Titicaca area in Bolivia." She riffled through the pictures of snow and ice and stopped, several pages later, at an article that Starbright had not read. "I thought we had been talking about those peapod reed boats they use to cross Lake Titicaca. Oh. So you read the Scott expedition instead? Look, keep the magazine. I don't need it." She thrust it back into Starbright's hand.

Starbright realized that she and the woman were trying to connect through completely different memories. But there was one more thing she needed to see. "Miss Tietz, your brother's article. It was in a yellow envelope?"

"Yes."

"Do you mind if I have another quick look at it?"

"No, not at all." The woman went back to the cardboard box. "You can do that while I stow the rest of my luggage in the trunk."

Starbright opened the yellow envelope and pulled out some photocopied pages. The top sheet showed a design of Northwestern Native American art, and under it were the words *The Tlingit Raven. Tlingit means people, and the Tlingit society is matriarchal. The Eagle and the Raven are the two main family groups. Tlingit law requires that opposites marry, Eagle to Raven. A Raven and Eagle at the entry of a home is an indication of welcome or friendly greeting. . . .*

She flipped the page over and saw something about masks and spirit dancers. On the next page was writing about Tlingit herbs and healing plants. She did not look further but put the pages back in the yellow envelope and laid them on top of the box with the *National Geographic* magazine.

Lena Tietz slammed the trunk of her car and brushed the dust from her hands. "He's flying home in about a week," she said. "Did I tell you that?"

"I'm glad," said Starbright. "I'd hate it if Esther got really sick." She walked around the car to the driver's side. "Miss Tietz, do you remember us talking about the night I was born?"

The woman looked at her and then slowly shook her head.

"You were Esther Connor's midwife. You helped me into the world in Bannerville, the sixth of December, 1986."

"Oh! Did I?" Lena Tietz's face brightened. "Well, you must have been one of my last deliveries. I had retired from obstetrics by then, you know. Not that I disliked being a midwife. On the contrary, babies are so healthy and normal. A nurse gets tired of sickness. Well, I suppose I'd better be on my way. It's been nice talking to you, Starbright."

"You told me I was the overlay," Starbright said.

This time, there a reaction. Something flickered in the woman's brown-green eyes, just for a second, and then it was gone. She stood there, looking empty and puzzled.

"It's all right," said Starbright. "It doesn't matter."

Lena Tietz took off her glasses and wiped them. "I haven't been well," she said. "It's been a lost week, I guess, but when you're retired, time is not so important. I shall enjoy the rest of my vacation. Good-bye, Starbright."

"Good-bye, Miss Tietz."

She watched the small green car turn out of the motel parking lot, and even when it had gone, she stood there for a long time, gazing at the road. The feeling of stillness in her was amazing. The morning sun was spread like butter over everything, and the air was thick with scents of flowers freshened by a sprinkler. Near her, some sparrows picked insects out of a car radiator grille. Farther away, two boys laughed as they flicked their skateboards up and down the sidewalk.

It had happened. The overlay. The Dream Eater had gone. Time had wound itself back in a split second and then, just as fast, had unwound in a completely different direction. The new time, the overlay, was now history.

She stretched her arms in the air and breathed deep. Hoo-diddly! This planet was beautiful! It was, it was! Scrumdeliciously fantastic. Like the whole earth was this amazing little ball that she could bounce and catch and hold against her heart.

"Yee-ee-ah! Lovesee!" she yelled, leaping high into the air. Then she ran like the wind in the direction of home.

JOY COWLEY is the award-winning author of over forty books for children and young adults, including *The Silent One*, which the *New York Times* Educational Supplement hailed as a book that "will not be forgotten," and *The Horn Book* called "brilliantly evocative." *Starbright and the Dream Eater* won the Junior Fiction award in New Zealand in 1999. Ms. Cowley is also the author of *Singing Down the Rain*, illustrated by Jan Spivey Gilchrist.

Joy and her husband, Terry Coles, have traveled extensively in North America and Asia. Their recent travels took them to Antarctica, a continent that has always fascinated Joy (and also figures in this novel). The author lives in New Zealand with her husband, a dog, a goose, a few goats, several hens, many cats, and even more sheep.